ALSO BY SARAH READY

Stand Alone Romances:

The Fall in Love Checklist

Hero Ever After

Josh and Gemma Make a Baby

Soul Mates in Romeo Romance Series:

Chasing Romeo

Love Not at First Sight

Romance by the Book

Love, Artifacts, and You

Married by Sunday

Stand Alone Novella:

Love Letters

Find these books and more by Sarah Ready at:

www.sarahready.com/romance-books

Sign up to receive bonus content, exclusive epilogues and more
at: www.sarahready.com/newsletter

PRIDE, PREJUDICE, AND FLIP-FLOPS

Fun-loving Isla Waterstone loves her laid-back life on Mariposa Island.

She has everything she could ever want...a great job as a journalist for the local paper, amazing friends, and pink sand beaches with stunning tropical sunsets.

The only problem with tiny tropical islands? There are more sea turtles than single men.

So when British billionaire Declan Fox and his aristocratic friend arrive, Isla's friends know this can mean only one thing.

Marriage.

After all, it's a truth universally acknowledged, when a single billionaire travels to a tropical island, he must be in want of a wife.

But Isla isn't convinced. Especially because Declan is the most rude, arrogant, prideful man she's ever met.

Or is he?

once upon an
ISLAND

SARAH READY

CROWN

W.W. CROWN BOOKS
An imprint of Swift & Lewis Publishing LLC
www.wwcrown.com

Copyright © 2021 by Sarah Ready
Published by W.W. Crown Books an Imprint of Swift & Lewis Publishing,
LLC, Lowell, MI USA
Cover Illustration & Design: Elizabeth Turner Stokes

Library of Congress Control Number: 2022905796
ISBN: 978-1-954007-34-5 (eBook)
ISBN: 978-1-954007-35-2 (pbk)
ISBN: 978-1-954007-37-6 (large print)
ISBN: 978-1-954007-36-9 (hbk)

once upon an
ISLAND

1

IT'S VALENTINE'S DAY.

I had big plans. I was going to lay on the couch in my underwear, eat a tub of double fudge brownie ice cream, and watch *Gentlemen Prefer Blondes*.

That's my annual tradition, started three years ago, after Theo and I broke up and I realized Valentine's Day sucks when you're single.

However, my tradition has been hijacked.

I wobble on my incredibly high, incredibly narrow wedge heels and readjust my gold sequin rose-colored sari. It's Bollywood brunch on the beach at The Pier, an upscale beachfront restaurant that hosts extravagant themed Sunday brunches with champagne towers, free-flowing mimosas and lots of gourmet mini-bites.

Kate texted this morning. All it said was, "The Pier at eleven. Put some clothes on, you sad sack."

Luckily, The Pier reuses themes, so I had a sari from

the last eight Bollywood brunches we've been to. I walk down the sandy path to the beach. It's shaded by a line of sea grapes and palms. There's a slight breeze today, which carries the salty scent of the sea and the smell of grilled fish. I stop when I spy the white tent set up for brunch.

Oh no.

"Got it wrong, didn't you?"

It's Renee.

She's best friends with me, Arya and Kate. Renee is half-Bajan, half-Trinidadian and a lawyer at one of the top international firms on the island. She works ninety hours every week and from what I can tell, she never sleeps. Every year, a young lawyer at her firm cracks under the pressure, and then Renee gets another promotion. She's smart, Type A, and loves to argue. She's also wearing a buttoned up white collared shirt that hits mid-thigh, white socks, a pair of black plastic sunglasses and nothing else.

"It's the 80s Tom Cruise brunch? Not Bollywood?"

"Bollywood was last week." She smirks at my sari.

Ugh. I wobble on my wedges. "Whatever. I'm Bollywood Nicole Kidman in *Days of Thunder*."

Renee snorts.

Then we see Arya and Kate waving from a table near the champagne tower under The Pier's white tent. The brunch is packed with people. The champagne has already started to flow and the band is playing *Kokomo* by the Beach Boys. I pull out a folding chair next to Kate and plop down.

Kate's wearing the bathing suit Elisabeth Shue wore in

Cocktail. She has two empty champagne glasses next to her and a plate full of half-melted chocolate truffles.

Arya is dressed in a bikini, aviator sunglasses and a pilot's jacket. A subtle nod to *Top Gun.*

I'm the only one in the whole tent not paying tribute to 80s Tom Cruise.

Oh well.

"What are we talking about?" I ask.

"I broke up with Chet yesterday," Arya says.

She takes off her sunglasses and rubs them clean on the lining of her coat. She doesn't seem too broken up about the split.

"Why?" I ask her.

Arya is famous for breaking up for completely random reasons. For instance, she's broken up with her last three boyfriends for the following reasons: his fingers were too long, his favorite book was *Anna Karenina,* and he was obsessed with flossing his teeth.

Renee sits down next to Arya and says, "It's Valentine's Day. Why would you break up the day before Valentine's Day? You had a date. You like having dates."

Arya levels Renee with a serious look. "He claimed cereal was soup."

I think about this for a second. Then I decide I'm on Chet's side. "Cereal is soup."

"No. It's not," Arya says.

Renee leans forward, she smells an argument. "It is. Cereal has liquid and floaty bits. What else is soup but liquid and floaty bits?"

Arya's disgusted with us. "Cereal is cold."

"So is gazpacho," Renee says.

We're silent for a moment.

Then, Kate waves her hands. "It doesn't matter. Chet made Arya cereal for a romantic dinner and called it soup. He expected some 'romance' in return."

"Oh," Renee says.

"Eww," I say.

"Exactly." Arya nods.

Well, that settles that.

I stare at the crowd around us and then wave over a waiter to grab a few mimosas for the table. The breeze from the sea is nice and the tent is cool from the shade, but even so, the glasses have condensation dripping down the sides. Part and parcel of living on a tropical island. It's beautiful, but it's hot.

"How's work?" I ask.

Renee is the only lawyer in our group. Kate, a British ex-pat, is a luxury real estate agent and a sucker for any man that is bad for her. Arya's parents are from India, but she grew up on the island. She works as a naturalist for the department of the environment.

"I spent all week cataloging boobies," Arya says.

Renee smiles at her and lowers her black plastic sunglasses. "How many boobies?"

"Hundreds."

"Were they old boobies? Young boobies?" Renee asks.

"All ages, really." Arya shrugs.

"Were there any perky boobies?"

"No. There were no perky or saggy boobies," Arya frowns at Renee.

Renee snorts.

This never gets old for her. Arya studies the red-footed booby population in the Caribbean. She's a scientist and doesn't find the humor in it. However, Renee thinks making serious, science-y Arya say the word "booby" over and over is hilarious.

"My dad called this morning," I say, interrupting the booby conversation.

Everyone looks at me. I steal one of Kate's melting chocolate truffle balls and shove it in my mouth.

"How'd that go?" Renee asks.

"Well, he asked what assignment I was working on, so I told him I'm writing an article on the best brunch spots on the island."

Kate's eyes go wide and she cringes. She's the only one of my friends who has met my parents. My dad is a Pulitzer prize-winning war correspondent and my mom is an anthropologist. They met in a war zone where my dad was reporting and my mom was studying the rights of passage in an isolated people's group. My dad is from New York, and my mom is from the island. I live in the house she grew up in.

"What did he say?" asks Kate.

"Nothing. He was silent for about thirty seconds. Then he asked about the weather."

My dad has never been shy in his disappointment over my career trajectory. He thought I'd be holding a microphone and dodging bullets by now, not reporting on things like brunch spots and the best places to catch a beautiful sunset.

"That's fifteen seconds shorter than the last silence," Arya says helpfully.

She's not wrong.

"Can we talk about how we're all dateless, sad sacking it at the 80s Tom Cruise Valentine's Day brunch for singles?" asks Renee. "I need some stress relief, and I'm looking at him."

She points to a late-twenties guy with a beer gut. He's wearing a tropical shirt and short shorts, dancing on top of a table, pretending to mix drinks like Tom Cruise in the movie *Cocktail*.

Renee doesn't date, she "stress relieves" for a night or a weekend.

It's intense.

We all turn back to the table. There's a pretty bouquet with a bird of paradise, some pink orchids, and a heart balloon as the centerpiece.

I grab another chocolate ball.

"I have news," Kate says.

She flags down a waiter and we all grab a glass of champagne.

I shoo away a grackle, the little black birds that opportunistically try to grab food when you're not looking. We don't have any food except chocolate at our table. It hops away across the pink sand.

"What's your news?" I ask, turning back to Kate.

She grins at us and spreads her arms wide. "There's a billionaire on the island." She says the word "billionaire" like you'd say "holy grail."

We stare at her for a moment.

"What does that have to do with us?" asks Renee.

"He's single," Kate says with a great amount of relish.

"And?" I ask.

"And in his thirties."

I sigh. "And?"

"And one of us is going to land him," she ends with a flourish.

I shake my head. Why did I come today? Why didn't I ignore the text and stay lounging in my undies eating buckets of ice cream?

"He probably clips his toenails at the dinner table," Arya says.

We all stare at her, but she just shrugs. "I have a list of all the fatal flaws my boyfriends have had. The automatic breakup flaws. That one is the worst, but it comes up surprisingly often."

"You're too picky," Kate says. "This guy is the white whale of dating and marriage. If he clipped his toenails at the dinner table and then sprinkled them on my food like parmesan cheese gratings I'd still marry him. I want one of us to catch him."

"That's disgusting," I say. "Also, I'm leery of white whales. Didn't Captain Ahab die trying to catch Moby Dick? He died...trying to catch a dick. Think about that."

But Renee has a bigger issue with Kate's statement. "Why do you assume he's looking for a woman? And why do you assume any of us want to get married?"

She has a point. I grab the last truffle ball. These things are delicious.

Kate gives us all a frustrated look. "It is a well-known

fact that any single man with millions or billions of dollars desperately wants to get married."

"That's not logical," Arya says.

Kate disagrees. "It's completely logical. Once a man has amassed a fortune, he's bored. Therefore he's driven to get married, so he can then divorce, lose half his money in the divorce settlement and then have the motivation to make more money. Once he's back on top and rich again, he'll look for another wife to give half his money to all over again. It's a cycle. Men like doing this."

I stare at Kate, completely aghast. She takes a long sip of her champagne and gives us all a superior look. "Trust me, I'm British."

I snort into my champagne glass.

Kate continues, "I saved the best news for last. He came with his friend, who also happens to be well-off. My mum called to let me know that Duchy said—"

Duchy is some duchess that Kate's mom is bosom friends with. Kate, despite living in exile on Mariposa Island, is from a top-tier British family.

She was supposed to marry some titled guy, but instead she ran off with a professional jet-skier. Two months later she dumped the jet-skier and wanted to return to England, but her parents had already disowned her. So, she stayed on the island, became a realtor, and continued to make terrible dating decisions. Five years later, her mom talks to her on the phone, but her dad still refuses to acknowledge her existence.

"Duchy said that the billionaire Declan Fox was moving to the island, and his best friend Percy Oliver is coming along for a stay. My cousin went to Cambridge with Percy, he's to inherit some title or other. I don't know." Kate waves it off as a non-issue. "The point is, one of us will land Declan, and another of us will land Percy."

"I'm out," Renee says. She leans back in her chair and shakes her head. "I'm not going to throw away my most productive career years on a man."

Kate looks at me and Arya. "La-La?" she asks me. Technically, my name is Isla, but Kate likes to call me La-La. "Arya? Are you two in?"

"Why would I want to marry a billionaire? Or some stuffy aristocrat?" Arya asks.

"To avoid that matchmaker your mom keeps threatening to foist on you," Kate says.

Arya considers this. Her parents are completely fine with her dating as many men as she likes, however, her mom is getting the grandmother itch, and she keeps threatening to hire a matchmaker. Arya's parents met through a matchmaker, and so did her grandparents, so her mom is gung-ho about bringing Arya onto the matchmaking train.

"Right. I'm in," Arya says.

I give Kate a pained look. "I just don't get the point in chasing after a billionaire and his BFF."

She levels her gaze on me. "La-La, you want to get married someday, right?"

"Sure. Of course I do."

Granted, I haven't dated anyone in three years, but it's not for lack of wanting. Our little Caribbean island has a serious shortage of eligible men.

Back when I was younger, I thought I'd be married by now, maybe have a few kids. But that was when I was a bright-eyed, nubile, early-twenty-something optimist.

Now, I'd love to find the right guy to grow old with, someone kind, and good, and who accepts me exactly as I am. But that guy is surprisingly harder to find than I thought.

Kate claps her hands together. "Great. Since the four of us are going to marry someday—"

"The three of you," Renee says.

Kate shrugs. "We can either choose to steer our boat toward toenail clipping, cereal/soup eaters, or we can navigate our boat towards billionaires. I've had enough dating disasters—"

"Here, here," Arya lifts her champagne glass in a toast.

"I'm tired of steering myself toward relationships that go nowhere. When I was talking to my mum I realized that I'm going to fall in love again someday. But this time, I'm going to only allow myself to fall in love with an incredibly rich man."

Hmmm.

I look around the brunch tent. It's getting rowdy. The champagne's been flowing for more than two hours, the band is now playing a tropical version of *Let's Get it On*, and some of the couples are cooling off in the calm azure sea water.

There are a few single guys here, most of them are in a group chugging mimosas. The one guy dressed in the tropical shirt that Renee pointed out is still dancing on the table pretending to make cocktails.

"Are you in, La-La?" Kate asks. "We can do this. By the end of the year, two of us will be married. One to a billionaire, the other to his well-off aristo friend. I guarantee it."

I'm a little tipsy from the champagne and the heat. I'm not really looking to land a white whale, but I have to admit, I am looking for *someone*.

"Alright." There's no harm in agreeing. It's not like we'll actually run into these guys.

"Excellent," Kate says, like it's all settled and she can start planning the weddings.

Even Arya looks excited. Apparently, she's really sick of the guys she's been dating.

"I'm going to go grab more truffle balls," I say. "Anyone want anything?"

No one does.

I stumble across the sand toward the food spread. It's never a good idea to wear high heels on the beach, you think I would've learned that after living here for years. But no.

I grab a plate and pick up a pair of silver tongs. There's a two-foot-tall pyramid of chocolate truffle balls sitting in a bowl of ice. I think about how many I should take.

Three? Five? Twelve?

I start loading some on my plate. Then I notice there are two men standing nearby.

They're handsome in that upright, British sort of way. The taller one has black hair, green eyes and wide shoulders. He looks like he could've been a boxer. He's magnetically attractive.

The shorter one is blond, with blue eyes and a slender frame. He sort of reminds me of a golden retriever, happy and friendly and approachable. They're both dressed in tropical shirts *à la Cocktail.*

"There's no need to leave. We're here to have a bit of fun. Mix with the locals," the golden retriever one says. His accent is posh British, similar to Kate's.

"I'd rather not," the boxer says stiffly. His tone is at complete odds with the ridiculous outfit he's wearing.

The golden retriever slaps him on the back. "Mixing is the best way to forget Vicky. There are plenty of good-looking women here to talk to."

The boxer looks around the tent aloofly. "You're right, there are plenty of women here, but I don't see any good-looking ones. At least, not good enough for me."

Wow. I take the magnetically attractive designation back. I'd rather date one of Arya's toenail clipping exes than this man.

The golden retriever laughs. "Loosen up. Look, right there at the dessert table. That woman there. She's good-looking."

My ears go hot and prickly when I realize he's talking about me.

I keep dishing truffle balls onto my plate and glance at the men from the corner of my eyes.

The boxer scoffs. "I'll pass. She's average at best. And then there's her face."

I stiffen. What's wrong with my face?

I have a nice face, thank you very much. It shows the whole mixed bag of my ancestors, perfect for the daughter of an anthropologist. My mom always said I have the kind of face that could visit nearly any country in the world and people would assume I was a local.

The golden retriever laughs again and shoves his friend toward me. He trips over his feet and stumbles to a stop in front of me. I look up, clear my throat and smile tightly at him.

Pretend you didn't hear him, I tell myself.

"Err, hello," he says. He straightens up and adjust his flowered shirt.

"Hi," I say.

He looks around the tent awkwardly and then back to me. "Nice day."

I nod, then hold the tongs out to him. "Did you want some truffle balls?"

He glances at the tongs in my hand and then back up to me. He's taller than I thought. Even in my heels, he still has a few inches on me. But he's also stiffer than I thought. I have no idea how a man in a tropical shirt and shorts can look pompous, but he's managing just fine. He gives the silver tongs a supercilious look.

"The truffle balls look good, don't they?" I ask.

Why am I still talking to this man? Why?

His mouth turns down and he looks like he wishes he were anywhere but here, in this tent next to the turquoise sea, talking to me.

"I don't ever eat balls, but..."

He sniffs, and it sounds like a restrained scoff. "I'll bet," he says.

Oh jeez. Did I just tell this man I never eat *balls*?

My eyes widen. Out of the corner of my eye I see the man's friend gesturing that he should ask me to dance. The boxer sees him too, he glares at him and sharply jerks his head no.

The friend walks over and pulls him to the side.

"Ask her to dance," he cajoles.

"No," the boxer replies.

"Ask her."

"I will not. I won't dance with some sad single woman, who self-pityingly overstuffs herself with chocolates on Valentine's Day and wears inappropriate outfits to beach brunches. I will not."

I drop the tongs to the table. They hit the edge of the ice bowl with a loud clatter. The man and his friend glance up. The dark-haired boxer looks irritated, the golden retriever looks embarrassed.

I smile at them and as serenely as possible I walk back to my table. I don't look back.

When I sit down my friends stare.

"What?" I ask.

They all lean forward.

Kate whispers, "That was Declan Fox. You were talking to Declan Fox." She holds up her cell phone so I can see a picture of him from the internet. "You've done it. You've already landed the white whale."

Arya looks at me with awe.

I can't help it, I snort and then I start to laugh.

"What?" Kate asks.

"Why are you laughing?" Arya asks.

"I would rather date a toad," I say. "I'm out. I'm definitely out."

Declan Fox is *not* the man for me.

"What'd he say?" asks Renee.

"Hmm. Let me think..." I put on his disdainful, deep voice, "I would never dance with some sad, single woman, who self-pityingly overindulges on chocolates..."

Arya gasps. "Fatal flaw. He's an a-hole."

I continue in an imitation of his voice, "She's average looking at best. And then there's her face."

"He did not," Renee hisses.

"He did." I smile at them, and even though his comment stung a little, I cross my eyes, stick out my tongue and say, "Look at my face! Look at me, I'm hideous!"

My friends shriek with laughter. Some of the Tom Cruise devotees at the brunch stop and stare, but most just keep on dancing or drinking.

Finally, Arya wipes her eyes. She was laughing so hard she started to cry. "Isla, we really should've told you..." She blushes and looks down.

"What?"

Arya doesn't answer.

I look at Kate and Renee. Kate crinkles her eyes and holds back a smile, but she doesn't say anything.

"What?" I turn to Renee. She'll tell me. She's a straight shooter.

Renee smirks and then brushes her cheek. "You've got a little something. Right here."

I reach up. There's a sticky substance on my cheek. I look at my finger. It's chocolate.

"And right here," says Renee. She dabs her nose.

"Are you kidding?" I ask.

"And here," says Kate. She touches her chin.

I yank out my phone and flip the camera to look at myself. My face is completely smeared with melted chocolate. I drop my phone and stare at my friends in horror.

"You jerks! You let me go up there smothered in chocolate."

They all start laughing. "It was funny," Kate protests.

"Funny until the face police called me a sad, self-pitying singleton," I say.

But then, I can't help myself, I start to laugh too. Because I look ridiculous, and the billionaire turned out to be a real Moby *Dick*, and my friends are awesome, and coming to this brunch was way more fun than sitting at home eating ice cream in my underwear.

"Question," says Kate.

"Yeah?"

"Are we still planning to land the billionaire and his friend?"

I shake my head. No way. No how. "I'm out."

"Good woman," Renee says.

"I'm in," Arya says.

I give her a look.

"What? His friend could be nice."

I shrug. He could be.

"Well, it's not for me. I'd rather end up a sad, self-pitying single old lady gorging myself on chocolate then marry that pompous, tropical shirt-wearing toad."

"Too bad," Kate says. "He's practically begging you to marry him and then divorce him so you can take half his fortune."

I choke on a laugh and then shake my head. "No. Not even for that. I have standards to keep. I promise you, I'll never, ever date or marry that pompous, pretentious man. And that's the end of that."

This may be a small island, but if there's any luck in the world, I'll never have to see him again.

2

THERE'S NO LUCK IN THE WORLD.

None.

I roll my little fuchsia carry-on case behind me as I walk across the runway. I'm a little wobbly and slightly dizzy, but I swear that the two men standing by the small plane are Declan Fox and his friend Percy Oliver.

I turn to Kate and try not to stumble over my heels. "You said this was a girls' trip."

I notice it comes out sort of slurred. That's because when I got to the airport I took one of my super-duper prescription-strength anti-anxiety, knock-you-out-cold pills that I only take when I dare step onto an airplane.

Kate gives a little wince. "I may have agreed to show some properties to Mr. Fox."

"Nooooo," I say.

I start to turn around and head back to the terminal, but Arya grabs my arm and swings me back around.

"Don't worry, Isla. You can count boobies all day with me."

"I don't want to count boobies."

I try to pull away, but Arya has a ninja grip on my arm. Apparently, Renee is way smarter than me. She turned down the overnight "girls' trip" to Rosa Island in favor of working an eighteen-hour day. Smart.

Rosa is one of the closer islands to us. We live on the main island, Mariposa—we have the town, the beach resorts, the restaurants and the annual Ascia butterfly visit in the spring when thousands of butterflies fill our skies. It's magical standing in the middle of hundreds or thousands of butterflies dancing around you.

But the outer islands have that "you're alone on a tropical island" sort of charm. Rosa has about forty year-round residents, miles of pristine pink sand beaches, and a booby nesting ground. Perfect for a girls' trip. *If* it's just the girls.

"You tricked me," I say to Kate. "That's totally beneath you."

Kate frowns and pulls down her sunglasses. "La-La, there was no trickery involved. You have two articles due, an eco-tourism piece on the boobies of Rosa Island and a piece on luxury beachfront housing. This is killing two birds with one stone. You get to work on your articles and Arya and I get to work on landing rich husbands."

I frown at Arya. "You were in on this?"

She blushes, "My boss asked me to count boobies on Rosa. It's a work trip for me."

"I'm showing properties. It's work for me too," Kate says with a wink.

I scowl at her, but the effect is ruined by my swaying. My prescription pill to "fly without fear" is hitting hard.

Kate pats my arm. "Don't worry. It's just a trip to the nesting grounds and a few home tours. After that we have the whole afternoon and night to spend together. Just us girls."

"Ha," I say. Because if I know Kate, and I do, she's planned some way to get together with Declan and Percy tonight. That's fine. I'll just hole up in my room and work on my articles.

"I don't think you should chase after these guys," I say. "Just because they're loaded doesn't mean they're good marriage material. Remember how jerky Declan is?"

We all take a moment to stare at Declan and Percy. They're inspecting the plane. Percy bounces on the balls of his feet, pointing out features of the tiny propeller plane, looking way too enthusiastic for eight in the morning.

Declan, on the other hand, looks just like I expected. His arms are crossed, and he frowns and shakes his head, then says something that I'm sure is cutting. When he turns and sees us looking at him his frown grows even more.

"See?" I point out. "Imagine marrying *that*. Imagine having sex with *that*. You're trying to get it on and there he is, frowning at you, judging." I put on his deep clipped voice, "Eww, your face. You're not good-looking enough for me. I can only get off to a picture of myself. Here, wife, hold this poster of me while I whack off."

Arya holds back a laugh and Kate scoffs.

"I'd hold a poster for him anytime," Kate says. "Imagine. A billion dollars. Come on, girls, work and then play."

I sigh. My friend is mercenary.

We walk to the plane and I try not to trip over my own feet. If I'd known that Declan and Percy would be joining us I might have held off on the prescription. As it is, I'll just have to deal with the slurred speech, double vision, and sleepiness. It'll wear off in a few hours.

No problem.

A drop of sweat trickles down my chest. It's humid and the black tarmac of the runway soaks up the heat of the sun. I'm in a puffy tropical leaf-print skirt, a cropped top, espadrilles, and a wide-brimmed straw hat. I considered wearing khaki pants and a button-up shirt for the booby preserve hike, but decided against it. I figured I'd stay on the boardwalk. Now, I'm glad I did. At least, this time when I see Declan, I'll look cute.

I notice that Kate is in tight white silk pants and a cleavage-baring tank. I should've realized what she was up to when I saw that. That's not a girls' day outfit, that's her man-eater look.

Arya, though, is wearing her usual get-up. Boots, khakis, a long-sleeve polo shirt and a bucket sun hat. She looks adorable in a science-y naturalist kind of way, but it's definitely not the outfit you'd wear if you're on the prowl.

Good. At least she's still kept the sense she was born with.

"Good morning, gentlemen," Kate says when we reach the plane.

Percy and Declan turn to us. Declan's jaw tightens noticeably at our arrival, but Percy takes us all in and beams.

"Good morning, good morning!" Percy says genially. "Don't you all look fresh and lively. I didn't know this was a party. The more the merrier, isn't that right, Declan?"

Declan doesn't say anything. He glances at Kate, then Arya. When his gaze lands on me, I imagine by the tightening of his lips that he recognizes me. But instead of responding to Percy or even saying hello, he just lifts a single eyebrow then turns away.

Wow.

Isn't that special?

"Wonderful. Just wonderful," Percy says, ignoring his friend's rudeness. Maybe they've been friends so long that he no longer realizes what a jerk Declan is.

Kate gives us a proper introduction and we all shake hands, then Percy gestures at the plane.

"Shall we?" he asks.

The pilot, Jimmy, is at the front of the plane, running through his final checks. "All set Jimmy?" I call, hanging back as everyone else climbs up the ladder.

Jimmy is one of the few charter pilots on the island. He's been a pilot since the early eighties and has crazy stories about flying celebrities, famous bands, heads of government, and even people with *very* questionable backgrounds.

"Looks good," he says. "Perfect morning for flying.

We've got some weather later this afternoon, but right now, we're all clear." He pats the metal side of his plane and gives me a reassuring smile. "Don't you worry, Isla. It's all smooth sailing."

"What? Me? I'm not worried. I love flying."

Jimmy snorts. He went to school with my mom. But unlike my mom, he couldn't stay away from the islands. He's an old family friend, and the only person I trust to fly me anywhere.

He knows of my phobia, but he's nice enough to pretend it doesn't exist.

"Go on and get settled in. We'll leave in a few." Jimmy goes back to his check and I slowly climb up the steps to the plane.

There are only five passenger seats. I thought I'd be sitting up front by Jimmy. That way Arya and Kate could sit with Declan and Percy. Instead, Kate has already claimed the front seat. Arya and Percy are sitting across from each other.

"Tell me more about the booby habitat, this is fascinating. I often go bird watching on the Farne Islands. I love the puffins," Percy says.

Arya has that happy-place gleam on her face that tells me she's found someone to share her love of birds with.

"I've always wanted to go there. Was it amazing?" Arya asks.

"It is. It was. We should go," Percy says enthusiastically. Then his eyes widen when he realizes what he said.

Arya doesn't notice. She launches into in explanation about the nesting location on Rosa island.

I smile to myself. I guess Kate did good after all. Arya and Percy are really hitting it off.

I scoot past them to the last two seats at the back of the plane. I shove my carry-on under the seat and plop down next to Declan.

He has out his phone and he's intently reading something, completely ignoring me and everyone else.

Jimmy starts the propeller and the noise fills the cabin. Percy and Arya lean closer together to continue their conversation. When Jimmy starts moving the plane forward I close my eyes, but unfortunately, my head spins so much that I have to open them again.

When I do, I notice Declan staring at me.

"Yes?" I ask.

He scowls. "You made a noise."

I probably did. In fact, I imagine it was a noise like "please, oh please, please fly okay."

"I'm fine," I say.

Declan looks down at my hands and makes a disbelieving noise. I look down too. I'm gripping the seats and my knuckles have turned white.

The plane bumps down the runway and my stomach flips with each little bump.

"Are you afraid to fly?" asks Declan. He has a judgy look on his face. "How can you live on an island and be afraid of flying? Don't you have to fly to go anywhere else in the world?"

I glare at him. His people skills are terrible. "I'm not afraid of flying."

He makes another disbelieving noise.

"I'm not," I say.

"Just like you don't eat balls very often," he says. Then he smirks at me.

I gasp and my back goes poker straight. I wasn't one hundred percent sure he remembered me, or recognized me from the Valentine's Day Brunch, but I am now.

"It's none of your business how often I eat balls," I hiss at him. Then I flush. "And I'm talking about chocolate, you...you...*man*." My insult falls flat. It's hard to be eloquent when you're drugged up and terrified of flying.

"I know what you're up to," he says, and his lip curls in a villain-ish sort of way.

What's he talking about?

"You don't know anything," I say. Because...comebacks.

He shakes his head and looks at me like I'm the larva of a slug. "I heard your friends talking in the terminal. 'Land the white whale. Nab a billionaire. Blah blah blah.' Trust me, *La-La*. I've had enough gold diggers after me to recognize one from a mile away. I'm not interested."

My mouth drops open and I try to formulate a comeback. Instead, all I manage are little choking noises of outrage. Finally, I say, "I'm not a dold gigger..." I shake my head. That wasn't right. Darn prescription. "Gold digger," I correct.

Declan snorts and turns back to his phone, effectively dismissing me.

However, I'm a person, not a dog he can dismiss or beckon at his convenience. So I lean over and forcefully poke his arm with my pointer finger.

He glances up and gives me an affronted look. "Yes?"

"I'm not a gold digger," I say again.

"Methinks thou protesteth too much."

I shake my fuddled head. "I just want to set the record straight. I wouldn't chase you, lust after you, date you, or marry you, even if you and I were stranded on a deserted island together, or if you were the last man on earth. Billionaire or bankrupt, I don't care. Because I don't like you. Got it? I don't like you."

Declan gives me a tight-lipped smile. "The feeling's mutual," he says. "Now, if you'll excuse me, I have important things to do."

Implying that I'm not important.

Well.

"So do I," I say.

I resist the urge to stick out my tongue.

What a jerk.

I turn away from him, my head spinning. When I look out the little oval window next to my seat, I see with surprise that we're high in the sky, soaring over the azure-colored sea. I was so distracted by Declan that I forgot about my terror over take-off, and my fear of flying.

I look down and make out the white sail of a sailboat, the dark greenish-black smudges of a reef, and a tiny uninhabited island.

I glance over at Declan. It's amazing. It seems that my complete and utter loathing and fear of flying was finally wiped out. I don't need anti-anxiety medication, therapy, or any other tricks. I just need to replace it with an even greater loathing – that of Declan Fox.

I grin gleefully. At that moment he looks up, sees my

expression and scowls at me.

Amazing. Wonderful.

"It's not going to work. You're not pretty enough to tempt me. Nor are you eloquent or smart enough. Or friendly enough for that matter. Even when you smile. You can stop trying," he says grumpily.

This makes me smile even more.

He's awful, and that's wonderful.

"You're the worst person I've ever met," I say with the biggest grin on my face.

"And you're the most vulgar, greediest, average-looking gold digger I've ever met."

"Perfect," I say with a smile.

"Stay away from me," he says.

"Gladly," I say. "Except we're on a tiny airplane and then a tiny island. Where you hired *my friend* to show you properties. It's your fault really. Kinda hard for me to stay away."

I can tell that he sees I have a point. He could've canceled the trip or fired Kate as soon as he heard her rambling about white whales. But he didn't. So basically this is all his fault.

He frowns. "Stop smiling at me."

"Stop looking at me," I say.

He clenches his jaw and turns away to stare out his window. I revel in the dislike radiating off him. This is great. I've never felt so relaxed flying. Tomorrow's flight back will be a cinch. And he really is so awful that neither of my friends will ever get with him. After today we can kiss Declan Fox goodbye.

3

EIGHT HOURS, FOUR LUXURY BEACHFRONT HOUSE TOURS, AND a nature preserve hike later I'm hot, tired, sweaty and ready for some girl time on the beach.

Kate has other ideas.

"Look at them," she says, pointing at Arya and Percy.

They're standing under the shade of a whistling pine tree on the sandy edge of the beach. Arya points out the large wingspan of a frigate bird flying overhead. Percy looks at the bird and then at Arya. He tugs on the string of her bucket hat and gives her a happy, lovesick smile. Arya smiles shyly back.

It's sweet. Really, really sweet.

Kate gives me a satisfied look. "He's already halfway to the altar. What did I tell you? I called my mum last night. Apparently, Percy has an old pile in the country, a flat in London, and some crusty old castle in France. My plan is working beautifully."

"Hmmm," I say noncommittally.

I glance over at Declan. He's standing under a nearby pine, only about twenty feet away from us. His arms are crossed over his chest and he's frowning out at the water. The back of my neck itches, and I get the feeling that he can hear everything Kate's saying. Although, I really doubt it. He'd have to have super hearing. She's not talking *that* loud.

But just when I decide that it's in my imagination that he can hear us, he turns to me, lowers his sunglasses and gives me an irritated glare.

I flush. Although I'm not sure why, it's not as if "nabbing the billionaire and his friend" was my plan.

"I don't think Arya cares about that kind of thing," I say quietly.

I turn my attention back to Arya and Percy, they're scooting closer together and laughing, probably at one of Arya's science puns.

"I think she's just happy to find a guy under seventy that loves bird watching as much as she does. And he's nice, cute, and normal – so far, no fatal flaws. He's a good one. I think she'd take him with or without the castle."

Earlier today while Kate was showing properties Arya and I tagged along. I came for my article, but Arya came because Percy asked her to. She was supposed to be at the preserve all day, but I could tell she was already enamored with Percy and he was enamored with her. During each of the home tours they stayed close, talking, laughing and sending covert glances.

It was adorable.

Kate happily showed the homes, detailing every luxury – infinity pools, indoor waterfalls, temperature-controlled wine cellars, movie theaters, tennis courts, manicured lawns and pink coral sand beaches that gently slope to calm, tropical fish-filled waters.

All the while, Percy and Arya ignored the properties and focused on each other. Declan listened to Kate in a stiff, stand-offish manner, every now and then sending a glower my way, or a scowl at Percy and Arya's close proximity.

Then, at the nature preserve, Kate stayed in the rental car while Arya, Percy, Declan and I walked the boardwalk. Percy and Arya counted the boobies, while Declan and I practiced ignoring each other.

Now, it's late afternoon, and we're all in our bathing suits, ready for a swim.

The beach is a little half-moon-shaped sandy area shaded by whistling pines. The turquoise water is shallow, crystal clear and slopes gently out to a small reef perfect for snorkeling. A mile out there's a little uninhabited island, about two hundred feet across.

Behind us is the cute little beachfront cottage Kate rented for the night. Unfortunately, right next door is the monstrous mansion she booked for Declan and Percy.

Well, not unfortunate for Arya, but unfortunate for me.

Declan sends another frown my way. I look down at my bikini. It's 1950s style with a high waist and a tiny top. It's orange and has little ruffles. Everything is covered up, no bits showing, and I'm not trying any come-ons. There really isn't any reason for him to be so irritable. He's on a beautiful island, for goodness sake.

Kate's in a string bikini, showing off the long legs and toned bum that God gave her. Her sunglasses cover more of her than her bikini. I smile at her. She's not subtle. I bet she plans on making her move on Declan tonight.

Good luck with that.

She gestures toward Arya and Percy, continuing our conversation.

"I know she'd like him if he had nothing. That's the trouble. If Arya has to fall in love, she may as well do it with a wealthy aristo. Me too. I'm falling in love with a man who has money this time."

I take a closer look at her. Behind the tinted sunglasses I see the worry in her expression. "Your mom really got to you last time you spoke, didn't she?"

Kate purses her lips and glances over at Declan. He's ignoring us now, looking back at the tiered stone porch of the Italianate mansion where he and Percy are staying.

"She said my dad is willing to forgive me if I marry someone...of the right ilk."

I frown, "Kate...that's..." Terrible, I don't say. It's terrible.

She shrugs, and I can't be sure, but I think her eyes are wet behind her sunglasses. "My brother has two kids now. I'm an aunt, La-La, and I've never met my niece and nephew. My parents are growing older. My younger sister is getting married this autumn. I want to go home for Christmas, have my mum's figgy pudding. I want to see my family again. I want to go home."

My stomach drops at her words. Suddenly, all of this makes sense. The focus on billionaires and aristocrats with mercenary single-mindedness. The "girls' trip." Kate turns her head, drops her sunglasses, and quickly wipes at her eyes. I pretend not to see. Kate has that British stiff upper lip. She's not one for displaying emotion.

When she turns back I say, "So, Declan then?"

We turn and study him. He is attractive, if you go for that bruiser-meets-businessman look. Or that scowling, broody look. Which I don't.

Nope.

Although I should warn her...

"You know, he heard you at the airport. He knows we're 'hunting the white whale.'" I finger quote the last.

Kate lifts an eyebrow. "Really? What did he say?"

I shrug. "Just that he heard you and that he's not interested in gold diggers and to stay away from him."

She narrows her eyes. "Hmmm. What was his tone when he said it?"

I think back to the conversation we had on the plane. It's sort of fuzzy. I fell asleep shortly after and didn't wake up until we bumped down on Rosa Island's runway. There was a lot of drool happening that I hurriedly wiped off my face. I remember Declan's sardonic look at that. But his tone...hmmm.

"I guess he had that superior, affronted, angry growl that he does so well. He was very convincing that he's 'not interested.'"

Kate lifts her eyebrows and then shrugs. "That's what they all say. But before you know it they're trussed up and in front of the priest ready to sign away half their worldly goods."

Declan pushes off the tree and stalks across the sand toward Arya and Percy. He says something to Percy and then pulls him away farther down the beach. It almost looks like he's giving him a lecture.

"That's going to be a problem," Kate says.

I see what she means. There's no doubt that Declan doesn't see Percy and Arya's developing relationship in a positive light. In fact, I imagine he'll do whatever he can to prevent it.

"You'll have to do something about it," she says.

What? Me? I turn back to her.

"What do you mean me? Aren't you the one trying to get closer to him?"

She plucks at the string of her bikini top. "Yes. I'm trying to *endear* him to me. You...he already doesn't like you. So when you frustrate his attentions to separate Arya and Percy he'll only dislike you more. No harm done. Then I can soothe his bruised pride with pleasant companionship, a beautiful sunset, and sex on the beach."

I raise my eyebrows. "This beach? Aren't there sandflies?" I swear I felt a few buzzing around.

I imagine Declan trying to have sex on the beach, all the sand grains getting stuck in uncomfortable places, chafing, the sandflies biting his bare bum. And him saying, "you don't tempt me, not at all." I flush at the thought, because he's not talking to Kate, he's talking to me. And he's posed on top of me, naked, while I lie on the sand under him.

Yuck.

I kick at the sand and Kate laughs.

"The *drink*," she says. "I'll make us the drink, sex on the beach, or piña coladas, or mojitos. Get your mind out of the gutter. Didn't you know? You can't catch a husband by giving him the keys to the pantry on your first date."

"Oh. Right," I say, and I shake out of the sand-covered, sandfly-biting fever dream.

"Are we agreed then? You keep Declan away from Arya and Percy for an hour or two, while I prepare nibbles and drinks?"

I frown across the beach. Arya looks lost and alone now that Declan has pulled Percy away. He's such a meddling jerkoid.

Well, that settles it.

Arya deserves a nice guy like Percy.

And Declan deserves to marry Kate so she can reunite with her family, and then he deserves losing half his fortune when she divorces him for being a jerk.

And it all begins with me keeping him away from Percy and Arya for an hour. No problem.

"Alright, I'll take care of it," I say. I lift my chin and put on a determined air.

"That's my girl," Kate says. She gives me a quick squeeze and then hurries off toward our little wooden rental cottage.

I let out a long breath, and my bangs blow high before settling back down to my forehead.

Well, here goes nothing.

4

Hatching a plan on the spot to distract a surly billionaire isn't as easy as it sounds. But Arya's slumped shoulders give me plenty of motivation. She's too nice to bust in on Declan and Percy's pow-wow. But I'm not.

I stalk across the beach, kicking up the soft sand behind me. Usually, I'd appreciate the feel of the sand between my toes, honestly, it's so fine it's like powdered sugar, but right now, I've got a job to do.

Declan and Percy are about fifty feet down the beach, their conversation is drowned out by the waves, but as I get closer I catch a few phrases. Most notably, "unsuitable," "devious," and "fortune hunters."

What is this, the Regency period?

"Hi guys," I call when I'm only a few feet away.

Percy turns and gives me a relieved look. His nose and cheeks are a little pink from the sun, even though he's smeared in sunscreen.

Blond hair, blue eyes and fair skin do not do well this close to the equator.

"Percy, you should put a hat on," I say. "I think I saw a few extra panama hats in our cottage's entryway if you need one."

I nod my head back down the beach toward Arya.

His eyes light in understanding. "That's a grand idea," he says.

"What are you doing?" Declan growls at me.

"Being helpful?"

"Not possible."

Percy pauses mid-step, sensing the tension between us. "Err, alright, mate?" he asks Declan.

Great.

If Declan says no, then Percy won't go back to Arya.

"I need Declan's help," I say.

Percy smiles with relief. "That's wonderful. Declan loves to help."

I hold back a snort and manage to keep a straight face. Declan narrows his eyes on me, like he knows that I'm fighting back a laugh.

"What do you need help with?" Percy asks.

I look out over the sea. The little island sticks out on the horizon, lush green foliage with a line of sand.

"I'm writing an article," I begin. I bite my bottom lip, trying to think, the taste of salt in the air tingles against my tongue. "I write for the local paper."

Percy nods, "Arya mentioned that."

Declan just crosses his arms and waits for me to continue.

"I have to go out to that island," I point to the little island across the water. "Just for an hour or so."

They both look across the water.

Declan turns back to me and there's a glint in his eyes that tells me he knows *exactly* what I'm up to. Or at least he thinks he knows.

He probably imagines I want to get him there to seduce him or something idiotic like that.

"It's not safe to go alone," I say. "Water safety rule number one, never swim or boat alone." I point across the beach at a little shed near our cottage. "There's a two-person kayak for our use."

"Of course," Percy says. "You need a partner. Declan?"

Declan scowls, which I take as a firm no.

Apparently, so does Percy.

"Or I could help," Percy says. Because, you know, he's a really nice guy.

I quickly shake my head. "No. No. Not at all."

"That wouldn't work, would it?" Declan asks. There's a mocking gleam in his eyes.

I shake my head. "No. It wouldn't." I pull out the perfect excuse as to why not. "Kate mentioned the island's included in the purchase price of the last property we saw. She said you should come with me so you can have the full property tour. To do your due diligence."

"Really?" Declan asks, doubt laces his tone.

He's probably doubtful because while Kate did mention the island is included with the property, she never suggested we see it. Still, he doesn't know that.

"That's wonderful," Percy says.

I nod and smile widely. "Yes. It is wonderful. Isn't it?"

Declan looks at Percy then down the beach toward Arya. Then he shrugs. "No thanks. It doesn't interest me."

He emphasizes *interest*, reminding me of what he said on the plane. Unfortunately, it also reminds me of the vision I had of him having sex on the beach. I flush and I know from experience that I'm turning beet red.

Of course, he notices. His eyes take on a satisfied gleam.

"That's a shame," Percy says. "Maybe Arya and I could go? We could take notes, pictures, maybe stay for a dinner picnic..." He trails off and both Declan and I can see the path that Percy's mind has veered onto.

A romantic, secluded, lovely path.

"I'll go," Declan says quickly. When Percy looks at him in surprise, he says more firmly, "Isla and I will go. It's for her work, and I'm obligated to finish the property viewing."

"Oh," Percy says, deflating a bit. "Well, I suppose, if you really want to..."

"Of course I do," Declan says.

He sizes me up, taking in my bikini and my oversized beach hat. He's in board shorts, a short-sleeved rash guard and a ball cap.

"I'll prepare the kayak if you'll get some bottles of water..." He pauses as he stares at my swimsuit. "And perhaps a more appropriate outfit for kayaking and exploring?"

Ugh.

Can't stand him.

I give him a blinding smile. "Perfect."

"Wonderful," he says back, with what I assume he considers a smile but looks more like a mangy wolf baring its teeth.

Percy seems fooled. He happily hurries ahead of us, back toward Arya. We walk after him, back toward the cottage and the kayak.

"Whatever you're doing, it's not going to work," Declan says through gritted teeth, keeping up the appearance of a smile for Percy's benefit.

Ugh. He still thinks I'm after him.

"Of course it is," I say, smiling too.

I loop my arm through his and he stiffens at the contact. His skin is warm from the sun. He glares down at my arm but I don't let go.

"And why is that?" he asks stiffly.

I look up at him and flutter my eyelashes. "Because it already *has* worked. You've already fallen for me. It's just sad, because you don't know it yet. Your itty bitty wittle brain is having trouble assimilating what your stone-cold heart already knows. That you looove me."

Blah. That'll be the day.

Declan scoffs, so I simper at him and pucker up my lips.

"That'll be the day," he says, echoing my thoughts exactly. I guess we're kindred spirits in our mutual dislike.

"Don't worry, Declan. Someday you'll beg me to marry you. It'll be grand."

I flush when I realize that he's supposed to be asking

Kate to marry him. And I really, really shouldn't tease him about it, no matter how tempting it is.

I let go of his arm and hurry toward the cottage to change into shorts. I'm in so much of a hurry that it may look like I'm running away. But I'm not. Definitely not.

Declan laughs at my hurried departure. My skin tingles at the sound.

5

I'M IN THE FRONT SEAT OF THE KAYAK. IT'S A RED AND orange sea kayak, long and narrow, and it glides beautifully through the water.

Declan hasn't said much since we shoved off from the little bay. I packed a couple bottles of water and made sure the kayak had a pump, a radio, some rope, a machete, a whistle and all the other gear we'd need in case of capsizing or an emergency. I'm slathered in sunscreen and the coconutty smell fills the air and mixes with the fresh salty breeze.

I love being on the water, and sea kayaking is one of the most peaceful ways to experience the ocean. In fact, the Zen-like rhythm of our paddling has relaxed me so much that it's hard to remember exactly *how much* I dislike Declan.

You have to work together in a tandem kayak, you have to get a flow going, and keep the right rhythm, it's a silent sort of communication. Years ago my paddling instructor likened it to dancing, then Kate, being Kate, likened it to sex.

The person in the back is the "lead." Declan is in the back seat, meaning that he has control of our direction. He's steering the boat. If he decided to turn us around, head to the other side of the island or go in some other random direction, there isn't much I could do to stop him. I mean, I could make it difficult, but he has the most steering power from the back.

Not that it matters.

We're halfway to the little island and our powers of cooperation are a sight to behold.

The sea is calm, there's only the slightest breeze, and when I glance over the side of the kayak I see a school of bright yellow and white fish flashing by. The sun hits their scales and turns them iridescent. The small ripples bend the sunshine and send light dancing over the sandy sea floor. I don't know that I'll ever get over the fact that you can see ten, twenty, thirty feet down, like you're peering through a perfectly clear glass window into the sea.

I turn in my seat and smile back at Declan. "Isn't this incredible?" I ask, forgetting for a second that we don't like each other.

He keeps paddling, and I ogle the way his biceps bulge when he moves his paddle swiftly through the water. Wowie zowie, he's a looker.

His rash guard shirt is skintight, and it shows off his flat chest and the muscles of his abdomen. It's amazing to me that his outside doesn't match his surly inside at all, in fact, it's... "Incredible."

"What's incredible?" he says sharply.

I stiffen. Ummm.

"Oh look, a sea turtle," I say and point in a random direction over the side.

He stops paddling and looks down into the water. The boat slows. "I don't see it."

I pretend to look for the non-existent sea turtle over the edge of the kayak. "Oh, well. They're pretty fast."

Declan gives me a skeptical look and tightens his jaw. He lifts the paddle and sends it to the other side of the kayak. Little water droplets fall across the boat, forming an arc. We start moving forward again.

I turn back around and help paddle.

Unfortunately, the peaceful feeling from earlier is gone. There's an itch between my shoulder blades that tells me Declan is studying me with quiet intensity. I take a quick peek behind me and then turn forward again.

Sure enough, instead of looking out at the water and the beautiful scenery, Declan's staring at me.

I roll my shoulders. The island is only another two hundred meters away. We can get there, poke around a bit, and then turn back. I'll be away from him and this awkwardness soon enough.

To dispel some of the tension I'm feeling, I point out a frigate bird soaring above. "They can stay in the air for months at a time, not landing once, isn't that amazing?"

"Sounds exhausting. Or like they're trying to get away from someone."

Argh.

"And who would that be? The frigate police?"

He scoffs. "I imagine they're trying to escape the conniving clutches of the female half of the species."

"Oh, look. The island," I say, ignoring his jab.

The kayak glides up to the shallow waters at the edge of a little strip of sand. The beach is only about fifteen feet deep, but it looks like it extends around the entire island. There are clusters of coral rocks and palm trees at the edge of the sand. The entirety of the island seems to be a mix of woody shrubs and palm trees. Basically, it's a tiny little slip of paradise. The late afternoon sun has turned the water glittering blue-green and it feels as if we're all alone in the world.

I have to admit, if I had been planning a seduction, this would've been the perfect spot. The kayak bottom hits the edge of the sandy beach and I hop out.

My feet splash in the cool water that laps against the shore. I stretch my arms over my head and get out all the kinks from paddling over.

I notice a tree loaded with quite a few good-sized coconuts just waiting for me to nab.

Behind me, Declan jumps out of the boat into the water. He grabs the kayak and pulls it farther up onto the sand.

He walks up next to me and crosses his arms.

"What now?" he asks.

"I'm going to grab a coconut. Want one?"

His brow wrinkles and he looks from me to the

coconut tree that I'm pointing at. The coconuts are about twenty feet up.

"You're going to *grab* a coconut?" he says. He takes in my cut-off jean shorts, T-shirt and bare feet.

"Watch and learn," I say.

I jog over to the tree, grasp the trunk around the back with both hands and "walk up."

I've been climbing coconut trees since I was three. My mom nearly had a heart attack when she saw me, a tiny toddler, fifteen feet up, clutching a green coconut. I've been doing it ever since. It's all a matter of counterweight and grip. I grab one of the bigger coconuts and twist, it easily comes loose. I drop it to the ground, pick another and throw it down too. Then I scramble down quickly and drop to the sand.

"Ta da. Fresh coconut." I wipe my palms off on my shorts.

Declan gives me a stunned look, like he can't compute the fact that I just scrambled up a tree and dropped down a couple of coconuts.

I smirk at him, then go to the kayak and pull the small machete I packed out of the storage hatch. I give the coconuts a quick whack and then carry them back to Declan.

"Cheers."

He grabs one and I knock my coconut against his and then tip it back and let the warm, sweet liquid slide down my throat.

Declan gives me a skeptical look, then takes a drink.

"Yeah. That's good," I say. I give him a sidelong glance. He's draining his coconut. Paddling is thirsty work.

We're barefoot, drinking fresh coconut water on an uninhabited island. The only thing we need to make this even more perfect is to actually like each other.

I drop my empty coconut to the sand and wipe my mouth with the back of my hand. Declan's eyes flick to my lips, then he looks away. He sets his coconut down next to mine.

"Thank you," he says stiffly.

His shoulders are tight and his jaw is still clenched. I have no idea how someone can be so uptight on a tropical island, but he manages perfectly. For my own sanity I need to find a way to get him to relax.

"Well, now that we're here my plan can begin," I say nonchalantly. I dig my toes into the sand.

His eyes narrow. "What plan?"

I look up at him and grin like a cartoon villain. "The plan where I seduce you with my coconuts and then steal your money. It's so easy, so fool-proof, you won't be able to resist. Bwaaah. Millions. I'll take millions." I steeple my fingers together and do my impression of an evil villain laugh.

Declan isn't amused. He lifts an eyebrow and then his eyes drift down to my breasts. He moves them quickly back up, almost like he's appalled that he even looked and he's hoping I didn't notice.

But I did.

"Not those coconuts," I say.

He looks away, but not before I catch him trying to restrain a smile.

Ha.

"Let's have a quick peek around then head back," I say.

"Fine with me," Declan agrees.

I head toward the little path through the foliage that I spied from the water.

"I heard there's a little stone gazebo at the middle of the island where you can have a picnic," I say, leading the way. The path was cut back recently, and it seems well-maintained. It's sandy, with short grass, and coral rocks lining the edges. The shade of the trees is welcome, and the farther we walk in, the more the air fills with a soft leafy smell.

The breeze has picked up and is shifting to a stiff wind. My hair blows across my face and I push it aside. The leaves rattle. I look up, but the little patch of sky that I can see through the trees is still blue. I rub my arms. The wind has a bit of a cold bite.

"Shouldn't be much farther."

"Right," Declan says.

His voice is nearer than I expected.

I look back, I didn't realize he was walking so close to me. He could easily reach out and touch my back.

When I turn back around, I see the stone gazebo. It's in a little clearing, with pink flowering bushes and little white flowers on vines. It smells like honey.

I walk to it and step under the roof of the structure. It's all stone. There's a little stone table with two benches in the center. The whole thing is about ten feet in circumference.

"Well, that's it, I guess," I say, spinning in a slow circle to see everything. It's charming.

Declan looks up at the roof and then around the clearing. Then he nods back at the path. "Have you done everything you need for your article?" he says in an impatient tone.

I wrinkle my brow. What's he talking about? Then I remember. I told him I'm writing an article about this little island.

"Absolutely, I'm all set," I say. "Have you seen everything you need to see?"

He looks around one more time. "I believe I have everything I need to come to a decision."

"Really?" I say in surprise.

Maybe this little trip convinced him to buy the last property. Kate will be happy.

"So, what did you decide?" I ask. Then I realize that's probably too personal of a question. I'm about to take it back but Declan answers before I can.

He shrugs. "It doesn't offer anything I haven't already seen. It may appeal to some, but to me, it doesn't hold any enticement. It's shallow..." He pauses and stares at me. "I prefer deeper water."

Holy unbelievable. He's talking about me.

He's insulting me. Again.

I narrow my eyes, then I decide to relax. Because, honestly, it doesn't matter. I'm not trying to impress him.

He doesn't know me, and I don't need to prove my worth to him. If he is so quick to judge then that's his problem.

"Your loss," I say.

Then I step off the gazebo. Right when I do, a bolt of lightning flashes across the sky and hits a palm tree down the path. The thunder that follows is a deafening crack.

I let out a sharp shriek and jump back under the gazebo.

As soon as I do, a torrential downpour begins.

Crap. Crappity crap. This must be the "bit of weather" that Jimmy mentioned this morning. This was why the breeze turned to a stiff wind – a storm was blowing in.

The rain pelts against the roof of the gazebo and the leaves of the trees. It's loud and coming at us at a slant. Even under the gazebo I'm getting wet.

I glance over at Declan. He's looking at me like the storm is my fault, or even worse, a part of my nefarious "plan."

"We'll have to wait," I yell over the deluge.

"How long?" he yells back.

I shake my head. "Fifteen minutes? Thirty?" It's hard to know, but usually late afternoon showers like this come quickly and then disappear just as suddenly.

I sit down on the stone bench and Declan sits across from me. We both stare out at the rain, agreeing silently on a temporary truce.

"I can't wait to get out of here," I say.

"Likewise."

I smile at him and he lifts an eyebrow in question. "What?" he asks.

"We finally agree on something."

"We agree on other things," he says.

"Like what?"

His eyes drift over my mouth. They're so intent that I lick my lips in reflex.

He doesn't answer my question. Instead he turns back to the rainstorm and waits for it to end.

Ugh.

I wrap my arms around myself, the rain is chilly and goosebumps form on my arms.

This storm better end soon. I can't even imagine what would happen if it lasted all night.

Nope. Not going there.

There's no way it'll last all night.

6

Oh no. It's lasting all night.

It's an hour past sunset.

Declan and I are still stuck on the island. The wind whips in strong gusts, the palm trees bend and the rain drives at us almost horizontally. I'm long past soaking wet and more in the drowned rat category.

We've been here three hours. Two hours ago Declan used his super-duper sat phone to text Percy and let him know we were fine, had shelter, and were just waiting out the storm.

I wrap my arms tighter around myself and try to stop shivering. Declan frowns at me.

"We could attempt to head back," he says, talking loudly to be heard over the downpour.

Another peal of thunder rolls over our little island.

"No way," I say. "I told you, the wave heights are going

to be intense. I bet you anything there's a small craft warning. We can't leave until this settles down."

He gives me a frustrated look. I get the feeling that Declan Fox isn't used to being told no, even by nature. I imagine that if it rains while he's at the beach he just hops on his helicopter or private jet and takes it to another beach where it's sunny.

"It'll stop soon," I say.

He doesn't look convinced. "That's what you claimed three hours ago."

Yeah. Yeah.

I shift on the wet stone bench. It's cold, hard and uncomfortable. And no matter what I hoped for or what I told Declan, I don't think this storm is going to lighten anytime soon. I start shivering again, so much so that my teeth chatter.

"This is unacceptable," Declan says.

"S-s-sorry."

He shakes his head and looks around the dark, rain-soaked clearing. Then he turns to me and holds open his arms. "Come here."

I lift an eyebrow in surprise. "Excuse me?"

His jaw tightens. "You're shaking. The rain's cold and not stopping. I'm warmer than you. Come here."

A flash of heat runs through me at the thought of walking into his arms, but that heat is quickly replaced with revulsion. Why would my body even respond like that?

"What are you waiting for? My offer isn't indefinite," he says. He starts to drop his arms.

I'm up and off my stone seat before I can think better of it. I hurry around the table and half-fling, half-shove myself against him. There's nothing graceful about it. I'm too cold and wet.

He lets out a surprised huff on impact. I sort of burrow against him like a mouse in its hole. I let out an involuntary sound of happiness. He was right, he's a lot warmer than me.

Mmmm.

Good.

He's stiff at first, but when I don't say anything, he slowly begins to relax. I've basically lost all inhibitions, because I drape myself across his lap and shove my bare arms and legs against his warm middle, then I drop my head to the heat of his chest.

He doesn't say anything, he just slowly lowers his arms around my back and holds me close.

I listen to the drumming of his heart over the rainfall and blink my eyes when raindrops blow into my face. After about ten minutes I stop shivering and start to feel halfway warm.

It's dark now. Really dark. There isn't any light from nearby towns, or buildings, and the moon and stars are mostly hidden behind thick storm clouds. My eyes adjusted after sunset, so I can make out Declan, the outline of the gazebo, and the shapes of the waving palm trees and the bushes, but I don't know that I've ever been anywhere so entirely dark.

I press closer to Declan and let out another shiver.

"Still cold?" he asks, then he briskly rubs my back and my arms.

I shake my head. "It's not that."

His hands slow and rest again on my back. "What then?"

"I don't like the dark," I admit.

Usually I wouldn't tell a near stranger something so personal, but these are unusual circumstances.

He makes a noise a bit like a grunt but he doesn't inquire any further. But, because the dark is pressing in, and I'm warm in Declan's arms, I decide to tell him what I've only ever told my close friends.

"My dad took me and my mom on assignment with him when I was eleven," I start.

He leans his head down, probably to hear me better over the rain.

"He's a war correspondent," I explain. "He wanted to show me the ropes. It was supposed to be a safe area, outside the conflict zone. He wouldn't have brought us otherwise."

I feel Declan stiffen, almost imperceptibly. I guess he can tell what's coming.

"The second night we were there, the moon was covered by clouds. It was so dark, when you turned out the lights you couldn't see your hand in front of your face. So, I went into my mom and dad's room and slipped into their bed. Ten minutes later, a militia attacked the village where we were staying."

I stop talking as I relive that night. Declan's arms tighten around me.

"What happened?" he asks.

I shrug. "Nothing really. The militia was driven out. My dad put my mom and me on a flight home the next morning." I smile ruefully into the darkness. "I was lucky, I figured out at eleven that I wasn't meant to follow in my dad's footsteps. And also that I don't like the dark. Two very important things to know about yourself, don't you think?"

He lets out a long breath. "You're right," he says. "It can take some people decades to realize they don't want to do what their parents expect of them."

"Hmmm." I lean in closer, enjoying the heat of him. "Is that what happened to you?"

"No. I always knew I wanted to start my own business. My parents fully supported me from my first endeavor at age five."

"What was that?" I can't help smiling. I can only imagine how serious Declan was as a five-year-old, telling his parents he wanted to rule the business world.

"I was the neighborhood messenger. I ran messages and parcels between houses for a fee."

"That's adorable."

"And successful," he gloats. "I made fifty pounds in my first month. That's gold to a five-year-old."

The concept of a parcel service sounds familiar.

"Do you own a shipping company now?"

He nods, and his chin rubs against my damp hair.

"It's an integrated shipping company. I own a fleet of more than six hundred container vessels. We offer services at three hundred and seventy ports in one hundred and sixteen countries. We're one of the largest operators in the world."

There's a world of pride in his voice.

I say the first thing that comes to mind. "That sounds like a lot of work."

He does chuckle this time. Then he says, "I hire incredibly smart people to run the day-to-day operations."

"Oh. Right."

"What? You thought I ran a worldwide logistics company all on my own?" There's a teasing note in his voice.

I tilt my head up to look at him, but I can't make out his expression.

"No. I hadn't thought about it at all. In fact, I don't think about *you* at all."

I think I feel him smiling. "That's right. I'd forgotten," he says.

The rain has slowed a bit and is no longer blowing sideways, although the palm trees are still bending in the wind. I've come to the conclusion I'm trapped in this little gazebo, in Declan's arms, for as long as it takes for the storm to dissipate.

I may as well make it interesting.

"What do you do for fun?" I ask.

He shifts on the bench and readjusts himself so that I'm positioned more comfortably against him.

"Buy private islands?" he says.

I snort. "I'm being serious."

"So am I."

I smile, even though he can't see me. "So, nothing

ordinary, like watching a rugby match, or having a picnic on the beach, or reading a good book?"

"I don't do ordinary," he says.

Oh right. I remember now. Mr. Fox is only interested in extraordinary things. Average doesn't *entice* him.

"Well, I believe that life is made up of the ordinary moments. It's the *ordinary* bits of our life that define us."

I imagine him scowling at that.

"I disagree—"

"Of course you do," I say.

"It's the extraordinary we remember. The big business wins. The awards and the honors. The perfect sunset. The exceptional first date. The rise to the top. The ordinary is lost in the exceptional. As it should be. A life that isn't extraordinary is a life not worth living."

I frown. I don't agree with him at all. "That's a really sad way of looking at things."

He scoffs. "Really?"

It's funny how Declan and I don't see eye to eye on anything. I'm not sure how to describe where I'm coming from, but I give it a try.

"Think of it this way," I begin. "Some of my most treasured memories are of completely ordinary moments. For example, I remember one summer my mom and I were lying in our backyard beneath the flame tree. I was tucked into her arms, she was singing and I was looking up at the bright red flowers filling the tree. It looked as if the world was a watercolor painted in bright, cherry red. Every time I think of that moment, I feel happy."

He makes a non-committal, unconvinced noise so I continue.

"Or, every day, my grandma would make rice. She would have me help her wash it. I'd spin my hands through the water until it turned milky white. I can still feel the grains slipping through my fingers, hear the sound of the rice swishing in the water, the tinkling of the faucet, smell the starchy scent of the rice. There's nothing more ordinary than washing rice. But the memory of it, the routine, it makes me feel content, and happy, and loved."

He's quiet for a moment, and I listen to the patter of the rain and wait for him to respond. Finally, he says, "What else?"

I think about the other ordinary things in my life. My job at the newspaper, my Sunday afternoons lying on a hammock under the shade tree reading a book, the evenings I used to spend playing chess with my dad. All ordinary events, but all mine.

"I suppose, by your standards, my whole life is pretty ordinary. When we get back and I go home, it'll be to my ordinary house and my ordinary job. But at my job, when I write that unexceptional article about the best brunch spots, maybe someone will read it and take their girlfriend to a place I wrote about and propose to her there. Or perhaps a couple will celebrate their fifty-year anniversary there. Or maybe when I write this article about luxury beachfront houses, a couple will read it and buy one and spend the next twenty years raising their family there. You never know what seemingly ordinary things can lead to."

I sit up and pull away from Declan. I'm warmed by my

passion for the subject. He drops his arms and I settle onto the bench next to him.

"I inherited my house from my mom. It's a wooden cottage, painted white with turquoise trim, there's a front porch with a spindle railing. It's nearly a hundred years old, the floorboards gleam from the decades of my family walking across them, the house creaks and groans with the wind, the rooms are tiny and the walls have cracks. There's a bookshelf in the living room my grandfather built. And the countertops are the lemon-yellow laminate my grandma picked out. It's an ordinary, old, island cottage. But to me, it's beautiful. That wood bookshelf is my grandpa's love. Those yellow countertops remind me of the Sunday dinners my grandma made. I'm fixing it up, all on my own, slowly yet surely. And you better believe, that when I finish it's going to be incredibly, boringly ordinary. Especially to someone like you. But to me, it's going to be incredible. All the moments of fixing it, and all the moments after. And here's another thing—" I poke him in the side and he jumps a bit.

"Yes?" he asks, and his voice has a funny quality to it.

I narrow my eyes and try to make him out, but I can't.

"Earlier, you thought I wanted you. But I don't."

He shifts away from me, and I suddenly realize how much closer he'd drifted toward me during my story.

"You don't?" he asks, apparently because he still can't get it through his head that there's a female in the world not trying to sink her claws into him.

"No. And even if I did, it wouldn't work between us." I'm certain of that.

"And why is that?" he drawls. His voice is as deep as the tropical scents coming up from the loamy rain-soaked earth. If there's one thing you can say about Declan Fox, it's that he's certain of his charm.

I shake my head at that.

"Because," I say, "I like the ordinary. The man I marry, he's going to like the ordinary too."

"Doubtful," he says.

But I ignore him and sink into the image of the mystery man I've been waiting on for years. "We'll probably start out as friends. We'll go to the beach together, go kayaking, go to brunch, he'll be handy with a hammer and he'll help me fix up my house, we'll watch movies together. All those ordinary, boring things. And then one day, when we're at the beach, watching the sunset bounce off the waves, we'll touch. Don't get me wrong, we'll have touched a thousand times before. Ordinary touches. But this time, there'll be something different. And it will have slipped up on us, between all those ordinary moments, that we won't have realized we had something until right then."

I'm carried away, all warm and fuzzy in my daydream of how I meet Mr. Right that it jars me out all my good feelings when Declan snorts.

I stiffen. "What?"

"That's unrealistic."

I bristle. "It is not."

He shakes his head and I feel his condescending air. "Your vision makes for the most boring, unsustainable relationship on the planet. That relationship will die of monotony in two years. Either one or both of you will experience lust or the excitement of love somewhere else and stray. It's clearly doomed."

"That's so like you," I say. I'm starting to get cold again now that I've pulled away from him. I wrap my arms around myself and try not to shiver. "Don't tell me you think the only kind of lasting love is the extraordinary, once-in-a-lifetime, dance-on-oceans-of-sparkly-magic, rainbow-scented romance where every moment is filled with excitement."

"Well—"

"Gag me."

"No."

"No?"

"No. I don't believe that."

Oh. Okay. "Then what do you believe?"

He's quiet for a moment. I can't hold it back, I give a big shiver in the cold of the continuing rainstorm.

"Oh, come here," he says, and he pulls me to him again. When he wraps his arms around me I melt into his side. When I do, he says firmly, "Don't get any ideas."

"Don't worry."

Thunder rumbles and a flash of lightning lights the gazebo for half a second. I see his lips lift in a sardonic, half-smile at my response. Then we're left in darkness again and I can't see his face.

"I believe in love at first sight," he says.

I shift in surprise. I'd almost forgotten my question. "You? You believe in love at first sight?"

"Why not?" he asks, and he sounds affronted.

"Well, forgive me if I'm wrong, but you seem a little cynical for that sort of thing."

"We all have flaws," he says sardonically.

I give a short laugh. "Yeah. I guess so."

I grin and lean closer into him. I'm warming up again. We settle into a comfortable silence, listening to the rain, the thunder, and the wind.

Finally, I say, "I don't really think love at first sight exists. I'm more practical. Has it ever happened for you?" Then I get all prickly and embarrassed although I'm not sure why. I try not to squirm in his arms and instead stay still and wait for his answer.

His muscles tense beneath me, and I wonder why I even thought to ask such a personal question.

"Never mi—"

"Once," he says.

We speak at the same time. I bite my lip and wait for him to say more but he doesn't.

"Didn't work out?" I finally ask, because even though I only work at the local paper, I still have that natural curiosity peculiar to journalists.

After a moment Declan lets out a sigh and his muscles relax.

"I don't know," he says. "She wasn't who I thought she was. It made me act..." He pauses then says, "Cynically."

I hear the smile in his voice when he calls himself cynical.

I think back to the first day I saw Declan. He and Percy were talking about how Declan needed to forget a woman.

"You're talking about Vicky?"

He grunts in surprise and then looks down at me. "What do you know about Vicky?"

I can barely make out the narrowing of his eyes and the tightening of his jaw.

I really put my foot in my mouth with that one. Embarrassment prickles over my skin.

"What sounds better? That I'm obsessed with you and stalk you and all your paramours online? Or, the truth, that I accidently overheard you and Percy at the Valentine's Day brunch? And I actually have no idea who Vicky is. Which one?"

He lets out a short laugh and I get the feeling that maybe Declan Fox (finally) doesn't think I'm after him and his mountains of money.

"I know you're a stalker," he says with humor. "Your machinations are so blatant as to be beyond obvious."

"True," I say. "Too, too true."

I smile out at the darkness. Declan is pompous, sometimes jerky, stiff and judgmental. But maybe he's also kind of alright once you get to know him.

Finally, I ask, "What time is it?"

He looks at his watch, the hour and minute hand glowing dimly in the dark. "Nearly midnight."

No wonder I'm getting sore. Sitting on a wet stone bench for hours isn't the most comfortable thing in the world. Even when you're held by an accommodating, warm man.

"It's not going to stop," I say, and I can't keep the disappointment out of my voice. I really was looking forward to a bed.

"No," he agrees simply.

"What do you think about sleeping? We could try under the table for a little more shelter."

I drag my foot across the ground, the stone is wet with shallow puddles.

Declan takes a moment to consider, then says, "Alright."

We pull out the bench and climb under the table. It is *slightly* drier, but the space is tight.

I'm not quite sure what to do now that we're down here. There's only a few feet of room to spread out.

Declan clears his throat. I'm guessing he feels about as awkward as I do. Then he says, "You'll stay dry if you lie on top of me."

I can't help it, my whole body flushes and I know my cheeks are as red as the flowers of the flame tree. Luckily it's pitch black and he can't see me.

"It doesn't mean anything," he says stiffly. "I know you're cold. Getting wetter doesn't help."

I let out a long breath and wait for my body to stop overreacting. It's Declan Fox, for crying out loud. Not my dream man. Just because I haven't sprawled on top of a man for years doesn't mean I have to start getting excited.

Jeez.

"Thanks," I say, and my voice comes out tight and strained. I try again, "Thank you."

He lies down, and I awkwardly, with a lot of elbow jabs and knees to his stomach and thighs, finally settle on top of him. He's as stiff as a board, and I'm not much better. In fact, it's so bad it might be better sleeping on the stone floor.

"Declan?"

"What?" he says, and his voice is harsher than usual.

"You can relax."

"I am relaxed," he says. And he says it in such a tense way that a laugh escapes me.

"Aren't," I say. "You really aren't."

He scoffs, and slowly I feel his muscles loosening.

I settle into him and rest my head more comfortably on his chest.

"Thank you again," I say. My eyes start to drift shut. I really am tired. The heat, the rain, the stress of the day has all added up and I'm about to succumb to the inevitability of sleep.

"It doesn't mean anything," he reiterates. "Don't let it go to your head. I'm not interested."

Ah, yes. His obsession with avoiding gold diggers flares its head again. I yawn and then say, "Don't worry, I couldn't care less about your money. I only want you because you're hot."

He snorts.

"Warm," I correct.

"Right."

He rests his arms across my back and the sound of his heartbeat and the rain drumming on the palm leaves lulls me to sleep.

7

THE FIRST RAYS OF THE SUN FILTER THROUGH THE WET
leaves, splash over my closed eyelids and pull me fully
awake. I let out a soft moan and stretch my stiff limbs. My
eyes are gritty, I'm stiff, and even with Declan under me,
there's still a damp coldness seeping through me.

At my shifting, Declan blinks open his eyes and peers
up at me sleepily. His green eyes are only a few inches
from mine. They're more vibrant in the morning light, and
I notice that they're the same color as the deep green of a
shaded palm leaf mixed with flecks of brown and hazel.
They remind me of the thick tropical foliage in my
backyard—it's deep green, lush, and full of surprises like
butterflies, dragonflies, moths, and vibrant flowers that
bloom throughout the year. An ordinary garden that's
extraordinary only because it's mine.

He blinks up at me and the sleepy confusion clears
from his expression.

"Morning," he says and his voice is gravelly and deep and thick with sleep.

His black hair is messy and damp and his jaw is shadowed with dark stubble.

I have a feeling that not many people ever hear his voice sounding sleep-laced or see his jaw unshaven or his hair tousled. Probably only the women he sleeps with.

I grow hot at the thought and then I stiffen when I realize how I'm spread over him. My legs are tangled with his, my breasts are pressed into his chest, and my hands press into his shoulders. I look down into his eyes and feel my own widen.

"Morning." My voice comes out husky and thick. It always sounds like that in the morning, but this time, I'm embarrassed by it, because it suggests certain *things*.

Last night, I was too tired to focus too much on the intimacy of our position. I didn't notice how long his legs are, the firmness of his abdomen, or the width of his shoulders. I didn't feel how I fit so well against him. I didn't notice the warm, tingling flush that races over me everywhere we touch. I glance at him in surprise.

Does he feel that too?

Declan gives me a quizzical smile. "Pardon my rudeness, but do you mind...getting off me?"

Oh. Ohhh.

No, he doesn't feel it.

I scramble off him and duck out from under the table. I roll my shoulders and try to stretch all the kinks out. Declan emerges a moment later. He brushes off his

clothing and straightens his shirt. I look to the side and try
to pull myself together.

Get it together, Isla.

It's Declan Fox. *He's not interested in you, and you're not
interested in him.* Pull it together.

I run my fingers through my hair and arrange my
damp clothing. The sun is high enough now that the
clearing is lit by a greenish, golden morning light and the
flowers are starting to open.

Declan clears his throat and looks toward the beach.

I scuff my foot against the stone. I have the feeling that
once we leave the gazebo, things will go back to the way
they were between us.

So, before that happens, I say, "Thank you again. For
last night."

He turns back to me with a distracted look. "It was
nothing. Shall we?" He gestures toward the beach.

I sigh. I guess we're already back to the impersonal.

"Of course," I say.

The water is calm, all the waves from the storm are
gone, and the surface is flat enough to reflect the orange
and yellow of the sunrise. We paddle back through the
bluish-gold tinted water.

It's beautiful. Really, truly beautiful.

Although, it's hard to enjoy, because the entire way
back neither Declan nor I say a word.

And I wonder, which one's right, my first impression of
Declan, or my second impression, or neither at all?

Oh well, it doesn't really matter. It's not as if we'll be
interacting much after this. When we pull back up to the

little cove, and the cottage and the Italianate monstrosity next door, I help Declan put up the kayak.

When he turns to go, I say, "Well, that night wasn't too terrible. See you at the plane."

He lifts a hand in goodbye and strides back toward the marble stairs of his rental. I frown as I watch him walk away. There's an annoying pinch in my chest that I decide to ignore.

I turn to the cottage. I sure hope Kate and Arya had a better night than me.

8

"She's going to marry Percy," Kate says.

I quickly glance at Arya. "He asked you?"

Wow. Arya works fast. Her face infuses with a dark blush and she looks down at the breakfast table. She traces a shape on the wood. I narrow my eyes. The shape is a heart.

"Holy mackerel, are you serious?" I'm so surprised it comes out almost as a shout.

Arya shakes her head. "He didn't say anything of the sort."

"Yet," Kate says. "He didn't say anything yet. You weren't here. All last night they cuddled in front of the fireplace, drinking wine and sharing stories about—"

"Birds," says Arya. "We talked about birds."

Her blush deepens.

"I'm no dodo," Kate says.

I groan at her bad bird pun, but she continues, undeterred.

"Percy said you can come and catalogue birds at his estate anytime. He was practically begging you to take over as mistress of his household."

I scoff and lean back in the wooden chair. It creaks as I settle back. We're at the little breakfast table in the small kitchen. There are tropical print placemats and salt and pepper shakers shaped like fish. The table is next to a window that overlooks the cove. The sky is still pale morning blue.

As soon as I came inside I took a quick shower and then started the coffee maker. The strong aroma of the coffee beans, Jamaican Blue Mountain, filled the cottage and drew Arya and Kate out to the kitchen.

"He was not," Arya says. "He was merely expressing his enthusiasm for a shared interest."

I glance at Kate and she grins at me and winks.

It's pretty clear, Arya is sinking hard and fast.

"You really like him, don't you?" I ask.

Arya looks around the kitchen nervously. I know it goes against her nature to fall for someone so fast. She's careful, she's cautious, she collects data and then decides.

"I...I..." She frowns down at the table, then looks up. "I do."

Kate squeals and claps her hands. She's in a burgundy-colored silk negligée.

"I told you. I told you! What did I tell you?"

I smile and acknowledge her brilliance. Arya buries her face in her hands in embarrassment.

I take the opportunity to reach forward and take a long gulp of my warm coffee.

Arya and Kate are still in their pajamas, Kate in her negligée and Arya in polka dot shorts and tank, but I'm dressed in a bright yellow sundress. I may be exhausted, my muscles may be stiff, and my eyes may feel like they're being scraped by sandpaper, but I have coffee and a cute outfit.

And apparently, taking Declan to the island and spending the night in a downpour wasn't in vain.

Life is good.

I grab a banana from the fruit bowl in the center of the table and start to peel it.

"What's on for today?" I ask.

I take a big bite of the banana and chew. It's slightly overripe, and very sweet.

Kate narrows her eyes on the banana and then on me.

"By the way, when did you get in?"

I swallow and the banana catches a bit on the way down. I cough and hit my chest.

Arya stops tracing hearts on the tabletop and looks at me too.

"Thirty minutes ago," I say casually. For some reason my heart speeds up.

What in the world. Why the heck is my heart beating so hard?

I frown.

"Oh no! I had no idea you were out there all night. Was it horrible?" asks Arya. "Percy said you had shelter. I didn't..." She trails off. "You got rid of Declan for me. It's all my fault you spent the night with a man you don't like, in the rain, without a bed..." She looks as guilty as a puppy that just chewed up your favorite shoe.

I laugh and shake my head. "Don't worry. It wasn't completely horrible."

I take another bite of my banana, a hard chomp, and think about how unhorrible it was.

"Tell us about it," Kate demands. "I'll make a veggie frittata."

She gets up and starts digging around in the refrigerator. I think about the night, about lying on Declan's chest, his warmth, how we talked, how he maybe isn't as awful as I thought, about how it felt when we went back to formalities, how it felt when he walked away...

I don't want to share any of that.

So, instead I say, "It was uneventful. We got to the island. The downpour started within a few minutes. It was too loud to talk much." I shrug. "We spent most of the night huddled under the gazebo. I fell asleep pretty quickly. Then when the rain stopped we paddled home. Like I said, it wasn't completely terrible."

I take another bite of my banana to keep from saying anything more. I don't really want to talk about my confusion surrounding Declan, or about how I spent an entire night sprawled on his chest.

"Don't worry, La-La. Your good deed means you'll be a bridesmaid at Arya's wedding," says Kate. She cracks some eggs with a flourish and begins to whisk them together.

I look at Arya, "I would've been one anyway, right?"

Arya nods and gives me a sly wink.

"I have to put in a few hours at the preserve this morning," she says. The plane takes off this afternoon.

"Is Percy coming?" Kate asks.

Arya nods, so in response Kate starts humming the bridal march. Arya smiles, but she picks a grape out of the fruit bowl and throws it at Kate.

"Ungrateful wretch!" Kate says.

I laugh happily. Arya has an expectant glow that I haven't seen in years. The smell of sautéing vegetables and coffee fills the air, and outside the window the morning sun sparkles on the sea.

Kate starts up a discussion about her plans for piquing Declan's interest. Apparently she's going to spend the morning on a helicopter tour of Rosa with him. Then, this evening, back on Mariposa, there's a charity gala on the beach with music and dancing.

"And Percy will be there too," Kate says. "And I have tickets. Aren't you going, La-La, for the paper?"

"Ummm..." I think through my work schedule. That's right, my editor asked me to cover the gala for the society section. "Yeah. I'm going."

"That's perfect," Kate says. She slides the finished frittata onto the table. "You can be our moral support. I can feel it. Tonight Arya will get a declaration from Percy, and I'll capture Declan's regard."

I give both her and Arya a tight smile.

Steam rises from the cast-iron pan as Kate slices a knife into the dish.

Suddenly I don't feel all that well. My stomach is doing

a little protest dance, sort of how it feels when an airplane takes off and I'm holding tight to the armrests.

"Are you alright?" Arya asks. "Your face went pale."

Kate pushes a plate full of asparagus and parmesan frittata at me. "Eat," she says. "You must be exhausted and hungry."

I nod and pick up a fork. "Right."

"Don't fret," Kate says. "You can rest up while I'm out wooing Declan with the helicopter tour and Arya and Percy are out counting boobies. Later you can take your knockout pills for the plane ride. You'll have plenty of energy for tonight. It'll be fabulous."

She stabs her fork into a stalk of asparagus.

"Okay, Isla?" Arya asks.

I pick up my utensils and give a bright smile. "Sounds great."

I push down the conflicted feelings rising inside me. There's nothing to be conflicted about. Really, truly, nothing.

9

FALLING IN LOVE IS A LOT LIKE TRAVELING. THERE ARE MANY different ways to get somewhere.

The first way is to take the quickest, most direct route to your destination. That's the people who fall in love at first sight, or within days, or at most within a few weeks. They jump on the love express train and get to love fast.

The second way to travel is to have no destination in mind at all. You just enjoy the pleasure of going on a trip, so you hop in a car and take the meandering back roads, the side trips, the detours. You may eventually get to a destination, and that would be a wonderful surprise, but the pleasure of the journey is more important. That's the people who enter relationships just to see where they might go and who are pleasantly surprised by love if it arrives.

The last way to travel is by taking the slow route. The car or the boat rather than the airplane. These are the people who know they want to fall in love, are aiming to fall in love, but will take the trip nice and slow, just to make sure it's real.

I'm at the charity gala, and watching the couples dance, I'd say there are all types of travelers here. The fast, the meandering and the slow.

It's evening, the golden orange sun dipped below the water an hour ago and left behind an indigo-colored sky punched with diamond studs. The waves gently lap at the beach. The temporary dance floor is near the water's edge and surrounded by tiki torches. The scent of citronella mixes with the cologne and perfume of the party goers.

I'm at one of the tall tables surrounding the dance floor, scribbling notes about the gala, and taking pictures. Most of the women are decked out in flowing green and brown dresses. It's a tradition to wear shades of brown or green in honor of the charity – The Mariposa Turtle Rescue Center.

I'm in a Grecian-style silk dress with a slit to mid-thigh. It's a muted watercolor pattern of swirling brown and green and gold. I even wore makeup and piled my hair in a curling, twisted up-do.

Earlier, when I was getting ready, I applied and then reapplied my lipstick then rubbed it off and reapplied it again. Then disgusted with myself, I threw the tube of lipstick in my purse and told myself I absolutely wasn't taking special care with my appearance because I'd be seeing Declan at the gala.

I don't care what he thinks of me.

Obviously.

This gala is one of the largest charity events of the year, and the cream of the island is here. I've already interviewed the governor, the head of the rescue center, and a number of business leaders.

In fact, I've got everything I need for my article. I tap my fingers against the bamboo tabletop and watch the couples on the dance floor.

The jazz band plays a love song.

Of course.

Across the beach, lit by tiki torches, I see Kate grab Declan's hand and pull him onto the dance floor. He doesn't look happy, but he also doesn't look exactly upset either. You might say that he's wearing his usual stand-offish, affronted, slightly annoyed expression.

Kate isn't deterred at all. In fact, she's buying a ticket on the jet plane to love and she's hoping Declan will join her for the ride.

Of course, I already knew this. Kate hasn't made any secret of her plans.

She called earlier to tell me she was eschewing brown and green in favor of a bright red miniskirt and hot pink strappy top. She asked if Declan had proclaimed a favorite color during our night together. I told her that Declan hadn't proclaimed anything.

Kate didn't mind that. She said that all men like red, and she was certain Declan probably did too. Then she started to sniffle a bit, and I realized she was getting teary-eyed, because she said, "Just think La-La, if this works, I'll be seeing my niece and nephew soon. I'll go to my sister's wedding. I'll have my mum's figgy pudding."

"You're right. Wear the red," I'd said.

It was good advice. She looks amazing.

Declan has loosened up and is actually leading Kate around the dance floor. They look great together. Declan all dark and broody, Kate all bright and vivacious.

I try to ignore the twisty feeling in the pit of my stomach. It's the same way my stomach drops when a plane takes off.

Ugh.

"I don't like to fly anyway," I say to myself. "In fact, I hate flying. I prefer slower modes of travel. Kayaks, bicycles, walking..."

I trail off and scowl at Declan's back. He's in a tux and the black lines of his jacket fall perfectly over his shoulders.

"A woman after my own heart. I prefer long walks on the beach to flying as well."

I turn in surprise at the smooth male voice. I expect to see someone whose looks match the cheesy pickup line. A man with a loud, tropical bow tie, or an obnoxious smile or a skeevy leer. Instead, I'm stunned to find a handsome man in his early thirties with tousled walnut-brown hair, a self-deprecating smile, and an understated tuxedo. His hands are clasped behind his back and he's turned toward the dancing couples.

"Were you talking to me?" My voice comes out sharper than I intended. Probably because I'm still watching Declan swoop Kate around the dance floor.

The man's smile fades and he turns to look at me. "Sorry. I thought you were addressing me earlier." He looks around in confusion. "Weren't you? I'm the only one nearby."

He lifts an eyebrow and gives me such a humor-filled look that I can't help but smile at him.

"I was talking to myself," I admit.

"Ah." And he nods with such solemnity, that I immediately decide that I like this man. I like him very much.

"I'm Isla Waterstone," I say. I hold out my hand.

He looks down at my outstretched hand and grins. He takes my hand in a confident grip, "Michael Sherman."

His handshake is warm and friendly and I feel a connection with him. Like he would be the perfect person to go on a meandering, off-the-beaten-path trip with. After a moment he slowly lets go of my hand and squints at me in the dim, evening light.

There are smile lines around his eyes that deepen as he looks at me.

"I have the feeling we've met somewhere before, but I only arrived here this morning. Have you been to England? To Newcastle?"

I shake my head. "No. I'm strictly an islander. Well, and an on-and-off New Yorker."

He shrugs and then brightens. "Perhaps it's our mutual dislike of flying and mutual love of walking. Not many people share those two qualities."

I laugh. "Plenty of people share those qualities."

He chuckles in response and I take a moment to study him. His skin is roughened, I think he must spend a lot of time outdoors, and his short hair is messy. He's handsome in a quiet, ordinary sort of way, not at all in the overpowering, magnetic way of Declan.

That's good. I have no desire for overwhelming attraction. Ordinary is good.

I frown at Declan. He wouldn't agree. He claims you need excitement and that lightning bolt of love at first sight.

"Are you here with someone?" Michael asks.

"Me? No. I'm here for work. I write for the local paper." I hold up my notepad and point to my camera.

"Ah," he says. "That explains why you're staring at Declan Fox. He's certainly newsworthy."

I flush. I didn't realize that I'd been *staring*. Or that it was that obvious.

"I'm actually...that's actually...he's dancing with my best friend. I was watching her."

Oh boy, Isla, try and come up with a better excuse, won't you?

The music stops and Kate loops her arm through Declan's. They're walking our way.

I pick up my notebook and hold it in front of me only to realize that it looks like I'm using it as a shield. I fan myself with it, even though it's not exactly hot out.

"La-La, hello! I didn't see you arrive," Kate calls.

She grins at me, widens her eyes, and then subtly nods at Declan. Her cheeks are flushed and she seems happy.

They stop a few feet away.

"We were just dancing. Declan's an amazing dancer." She looks up at him with a sultry smile. "Is there anything you can't do?"

Declan scowls at me. "No. There isn't."

Hey. What did I do?

He said no in his short terse way. I notice that he's even stiffer than usual. His jaw is tight and his lips are turned down. He glares at me and completely ignores both Kate and Michael.

Well.

If he didn't want to dance with Kate he should've just told her. Jeez.

Kate clears her throat in the awkward silence that follows his terse pronouncement. Then she says, "Well...I certainly love confidence in a man."

Declan doesn't react to her announcement. So Kate sends an appraising look Michael's way. I'm sure she hasn't met him, since, like he mentioned, he's only been on the island since this morning.

I try to break the icy tension coming from Declan with a jovial introduction.

"Kate, this is Michael Sherman. Michael is from England and an avid walker. Michael, this is Kate Collingwood. She's also from England, although sadly, she loves to fly and prefers driving over walking."

I smile at Michael and he gives me a conspiratorial wink.

"It's a pleasure." He holds out his hand to Kate. She takes her arm from Declan's and gives Michael her hand.

"Likewise," Kate says. When she smiles her button nose crinkles in an adorable sort of way.

Once Kate drops Michael's hand I say, "And Michael, this is—"

"Hullo, Dec," Michael says.

I look at him in surprise. I had no idea he knew Declan. Well, I mean, it was obvious he knew who he was, because he asked why I was staring at Declan. But I didn't know that they were close enough for him to call him *Dec*.

"Sherman," Declan says. And even as accustomed as I am to Declan's usual stiffness, I'm completely taken aback by his cold tone.

"I didn't expect to run into you here," says Michael, apparently as oblivious as Percy is to Declan's demeanor. "Good to see you, mate."

In the usual course of conversation, it would be Declan's turn to say, "good to see you, too." But Declan doesn't do usual. He remains tight-lipped and silent, implying that it's not good to see Michael.

"Well...ummm...the gala's nice, isn't it?" I say lamely.

Declan sends a thunderous look my way.

What in the world?

I don't care if he is a billionaire and sweetly let me sleep on his chest, he's being a jerk. In fact, he's being exactly like he was when I met him the first time. Apparently, first impressions are more accurate than second impressions.

"Very nice. It's a lovely gala," Kate says.

"With even lovelier company," Michael adds. "I'm so pleased I met you. Isla, would you do me the honor of—"

"Dance with me," Declan interrupts.

He holds out his hand to me. It hangs between us, demanding my acquiescence. As if on cue, the band begins the chords of another song.

I stare at Declan in shock.

He stares back at me, his gaze unyielding and unrepentant.

Are you kidding me?

Did he just rudely interrupt when Michael was about to ask me to dance? Did he just *demand* that I dance with him instead?

"Sorry?"

"Dance with me," he demands.

His hand still hangs in the air between us.

Kate looks between us and wrinkles her brow. She's confused, but also too diplomatic to say anything. Michael shifts uncomfortably. I imagine he's too polite to say anything too. But by their postures, both Kate and Michael feel incredibly awkward and uncomfortable.

If Declan had asked me on the little deserted island to dance, if he'd danced with me under the gazebo with the rainfall as our soundtrack, I'd have felt a ping of happiness, maybe even a certain swooniness. After I'd opened up, and he'd shared with me, I would've danced with him. And I may have felt something in his arms. But that was then, and this is now.

And right now he's being a jerk.

Apparently last night was out of character for Declan, and he's back to his old self.

Michael and Percy may be oblivious to his rudeness, and Kate may not feel comfortable telling Declan he's being awful, but I don't mind. After all, I'm not the one trying to endear myself to him, and I'm not his old friend or mate.

"No," I say. And I say it in as terse and tight a voice as he uses.

Declan's eyebrows lift. "Excuse me?"

"No." And because it seems he needs a little more of an explanation I say, "Thank you for the kind offer, but as you've made perfectly clear, you aren't *interested* in dancing, and I truly don't want to inconvenience you. Thank you for the offer, but no."

Declan's expression finally shifts from cold and stiff to stunned. The look is only for a moment, but it seems that my rejection shocked him.

I give him a small smile. I don't want to hurt his feelings, I just don't want him to treat the people I'm with so rudely.

"Please excuse me." I nod at him. Slowly, he dips his chin in acknowledgement and drops his hand.

"Of course," he says.

And that's that.

I want to tell Declan that it doesn't mean anything, or that he doesn't find me pretty anyway, but none of that can or should be said in front of Michael and Kate. Or really, maybe it shouldn't be said at all.

Declan isn't my type. He isn't the meandering, slow-going, normal kind of relationship guy.

He's the high-speed train kind of guy and Kate's holding out a ticket to ride.

I turn back to Michael. "You were saying?"

He stares at me for a moment, a shocked look on his face that he quickly covers with an amiable smile. "I...ah...

was going to ask for the honor of…retrieving you a glass of wine."

Hah.

I'll bet my right foot that he was going to ask me to dance but he doesn't want to offend the curmudgeon known as Declan Fox.

Oh well.

"Thank you. I'll come with you," I say.

Poor Michael, a nice guy, railroaded by Declan Fox, cranky billionaire titan.

I turn and give Kate a subtle wink. She sends me a look that lets me know we'll be discussing all of this later. But I can tell she's happy to be left on her own with Declan.

I grab my notebook and camera, then say, "See you later Kate. Declan. Enjoy the night."

Michael and I walk across the sand toward the outdoor bar. We're both quiet for a few moments as we pass more tables and groups of people. There's a silent auction section with paintings by local artists, sculptures of sea life, gift baskets and packages for stays at local resorts or sunset sails.

I slow as we pass the art table. There's a sculpted sea turtle that's particularly beautiful.

"Just a moment," I say to Michael. Then I bend down and write my name at the bottom of the sheet with a bid twenty dollars higher than the previous bidder. It's still a low bid, although it's at the top of my budget. It's extremely unlikely that I'll win, but you never know, maybe I'll get lucky.

"You have good taste," Michael says.

"It's beautiful, isn't it?" I ask.

"Indeed."

When I look up from the sculpture I'm surprised to find that Michael is looking at me, not the turtle.

I can't help it, I blush. Luckily my skin is dark enough to cover any pink in my cheeks, plus the light is dim. Michael will never know that his cheesy lines affect me.

We start to move toward the bar again, and soon Michael has gotten us both a glass of sauvignon blanc.

He tips his glass to mine and it clinks. "To new friends and long, slow walks on the beach."

"To new friends," I say.

I take a sip of the wine and let the passion fruit and green apple flavor spread over my tongue.

We both turn and look at the ocean, the flickering flames of the tiki torches and the couples dancing.

To the west of the dance floor I spot Arya and Percy. She's pointing up at the stars. I smile when I see him slowly move his arm and place it around her back.

Michael clears his throat. "I'm sorry for any discomfort earlier, during my interaction with Dec."

I turn to him and note the chagrinned look on his face.

"What are you talking about? You don't have anything to apologize for. He was rude. He was intolerable." Then I feel a pinch of disloyalty because he's not always intolerable.

Michael grimaces. "Still."

Ugh. Apparently Michael isn't as immune to Declan's boorishness as I thought. He's apologizing for the discomfort *Declan* caused. Terrible.

"Don't worry about it," I say. "He's awful to everyone. It's not your fault."

Michael makes a sharp noise of surprise. "I've never known anyone to say that. Usually people are too much in awe of him to notice his faults. They only sing his praises."

"You won't hear me singing."

Michael laughs, and it sounds just like the wine tastes, light and zesty and happy.

"Are you staying long on the island?" I ask, suddenly wanting to continue our newly budding friendship. Michael is friendly, considerate and easy to talk to.

He stares toward the dance floor for a moment and I notice that he's looking toward Kate and Declan.

"I may, it depends..." He trails off.

"Because of Declan?" I shake my head. "Never mind, don't answer that. I didn't mean to pry."

Michael gives me that humor-filled smile that I think may be his signature look. "Yes. Because of Declan."

"Oh," I say, feeling crestfallen, and I'm not sure whether I feel that way because Michael might leave, or because it shows that Declan is a bully.

On impulse I say, "You shouldn't leave just because he's a stiff, pompous, pride-filled jerk. You have as much right to be here as him."

Then I feel silly, because actually, I don't know either of them. They both could be jerks for all I know.

Michael sets his glass down on a nearby table. He stares out at the ocean and puts his hands in his pockets.

"Do you know, I think you're right."

"Of course I am," I agree.

He rocks back on his heels, then turns back to me. "Dec and I go way back."

"Oh."

He nods. "We grew up together. Our fathers were best friends from their youth forward, so naturally Dec and I played together as children. Dec was always sulking, demanding, being catered to, you can imagine, I'm sure. His parents gave him everything he wanted. His family was quite wealthy, while mine was...not. Dec's father went into finance, while my father went into teaching. They were very different, but both good men. Dec's father was the best sort. Jovial, generous, warm. Unfortunately, the apple fell far from the tree."

I grip the warm handle of my wine glass. For some reason, the recitation of Declan as a child makes me sad. I remember him saying his parents supported him in every way, I didn't realize that was code for him being spoiled and bratty.

"So, you were friends? What happened?" I take another sip of wine to push down the lump in my throat.

Michael shrugs. "Dec had a business idea after university. His father wouldn't fund him, so he went to my father. My father gave Dec his entire life savings and all he had saved for retirement. Everything. With the understanding that they were partners in Dec's venture. Dec agreed. They signed a contract. Shortly after, Dec became successful, he reneged on the agreement and took everything."

It takes a moment for what Michael's saying to sink in. Declan stole?

"He...what? That's...but didn't you take him to court? Or see a lawyer, or...?"

"Dec had better lawyers." Michael smiles, and there's less humor there than the last time.

I set my glass down. I don't think I can drink any more wine. I feel slightly ill.

"It didn't matter much. My father died less than a year later. Dec's father demanded that he repay me for my father's investment. He demanded Dec make me partner in my father's place. Instead Dec gave me a pittance and told me to let it alone unless I wanted to spend years in court."

"That's horrible," I say. "All his success is due to your father? And he treats you like this?"

I glare across the dance floor. Declan and Kate are with Percy and Arya now. Declan stands a way off from the other three. While they chat and laugh he stands aloof and stiff, his head turned away, his shoulders tight.

Even my first impression was wrong. He's more awful than I thought.

"There's more," Michael says.

I quickly look back at him, "How can there be more?"

"I found a woman that I love and wanted to marry. Declan convinced her I was only after her money. He drove her away."

My eyes go wide. That rings with a horrible sort of truth. Isn't that exactly what Declan said to me? What he was trying to say to Percy about Arya?

Wow.

The earlier interaction with Declan and Michael makes so much more sense now. Declan really didn't want to be reminded of what he did to Michael or Michael's father.

"How can you be nice to him, after all that?"

Michael gives me a small smile. "I can be nice, because I realize he can't help being who he is. He was miserable when we were boys and he's miserable now. But, for the respect and admiration I have for his father, I'll always treat Dec with friendship."

Declan doesn't deserve Michael.

"What does his father think now?" I ask.

Michael shakes his head. "He passed shortly after my father."

I wrap my arms around myself against the sudden evening chill.

"I'm sorry," I say.

We stand silently. Michael stares at the ocean and I look toward Declan. Even though he's with Kate, Arya and Percy, he looks alone. And I suppose he is. I'd feel sorry for him, except he's too prideful and stand-offish for it to be any other way.

I'll have to tell Kate that she should forget about pursuing Declan. Although she said she'd marry him even if he sprinkled his toenail clippings on her pasta, I don't think she'd go so far as to marry an immoral, unscrupulous thief who purposely ruins people's relationships.

Finally, I turn back to Michael, one thought at the top of my mind.

"I think you should stay. Don't let the past ruin your present. I, for one, am happy you're here."

No matter what Declan has done, Michael is a nice, good person. He deserves to be happy.

Michael gives me a crinkly, cheery smile, and I notice again how handsome he is. In that perfectly normal, average sort of way.

"Thank you," he says. "Perhaps you might show me some of your favorite spots on the island..."

He trails off and I notice a slight reddening in his cheeks.

"I didn't mean to imply," he says. "You don't have to—"

"Of course I will. I'd love to."

We smile at each other. And I decide that yes, this is the beginning of a nice, slow trip that may or may not come to a surprising end destination.

Like friendship.

Or—

Like love.

10

"So, you're telling me that Declan stole an old man's entire life savings to start his business?" Kate asks.

It's Saturday morning and we're all gathered at my place for a painting party. My friends agreed they'd help paint my living room walls a nice, light, coral color. The shade matches the sea fans that wash up on the beach and the light pinkish orange interior of the conch shells that you can find in the rocky coves after a storm.

There are paint trays full of paint, rollers and brushes, and paint cloths covering the furniture and the floor.

Everyone is here – Kate, Arya, and Renee. We're all wearing the scrubbiest clothes we own. Cut-off shorts and old T-shirts, pajama pants and oversized tank tops, or in Renee's case, a business suit that she claims is three seasons out of style and can't even be worn to her home office.

"Scuttlebutt. You can't judge someone guilty based on

the word of another party," Renee says. She slaps her wet paintbrush against the wall and drags it over the old light yellow color.

"Scuttlebutt? Is that a legal term?" I ask.

Arya grins. She's the sloppiest painter I've ever seen, paint's splattered in her hair, on her face and over her clothes.

She shakes her head and says, "Renee's right. Percy respects Declan a lot. He wouldn't be friends with someone that did terrible things like that. He really wouldn't."

I hold back from slapping my head. "Okay, yes. We all know that Percy is a really, really nice guy."

Arya blushes and holds back a smile. She's sunk.

"What did I tell you? Arya and Percy are a match made in heaven. And it's all due to me," Kate says.

"Yes, yes," I say. "But back to the point, maybe Percy doesn't know about Declan's past. I don't think it's common knowledge. It's not as if Michael goes around sharing the news with everyone."

"But..." Arya says. She frowns. The paint roller she's holding drips a glob of paint onto her pajama pants.

I'm so glad we put down sheets and paint cloths on all the floors and furniture.

"Michael could've lied," Renee says. "People lie all the time. Even under oath." She scowls at the last bit.

"But why would he lie?" I ask. "There's no reason to. Michael's father lost his entire savings, then Michael lost his father, and then he lost the woman he loves. Why would he lie about that?"

Renee shrugs. "Let me meet him, I'll tell you whether he's a liar."

"Wow," Kate says. "Can I bring you on all my first dates?"

Renee flings a bit of paint at Kate, "No. I'm busy conquering the legal world. Besides, you like dating liars. They add spice to your life."

Kate wipes the spray of paint from her cheek. "I don't want any more spice. I want a stiff, uptight billionaire so I can go home. Is that too much to ask?"

With her put-upon air and her woe-is-me wail Kate sounds like a member of a Greek chorus from one of the ancient comic tragedies.

I can't help it, I snort. It's so ridiculous.

I hold my thumb and finger out and pinch them together, "Maybe a little. Like a millimeter too much."

I look at the space between my finger and thumb and adjust the width between them to a millimeter.

Arya stifles a giggle.

"It's not!" Kate says. She puts her hands on her hips and sends a mock glare my way. "I'm willing to put up with toenail clippings in my pasta."

Renee makes a gagging noise.

Kate glares at her. "And I'm willing to put up with an immoral, pension-stealing, uptight bore. He can nab grannies' purses and babies' rattles for all I care. I'll marry him, go home, be forgiven and then divorce him after a full year of 'irreconcilable differences.' I'll have a hefty divorce settlement, and I'll give Michael his father's savings back if you like. And every single one of us will have a happily ever after."

Except Declan.

Arya has a look of horror on her face. "Kate, that's...cold."

Renee shrugs, "Make sure you have a superb lawyer. Before the wedding. Get a consult. Have them on retainer."

"Good advice," Kate says.

"Gross," Arya says.

Kate rolls her eyes. "I don't have your lucky stars. You and Percy are a match made in heaven. It was obvious the second you met you were meant to be."

Arya blushes again. I wonder what happened at the gala, or after the gala.

"But just because I don't love Declan, and just because he may be a skeevy immoral bore, doesn't mean that I can't make him happy for a year of marriage. You'll see. It'll all work out for the best. He needs a first wife. Every tycoon needs a first wife so he can move on to his second, then his third, maybe a fourth." She shrugs like the progression of Declan's wives doesn't matter.

"Just to be clear, Declan stealing money and ruining relationships doesn't matter to you?" I ask.

Kate looks at me like I'm a simpleton. "Clearly not."

Arya still looks horrified. "But what if he hasn't stolen anything, and he's actually a good person? Then you're just tricking him into marriage and leaving him broken-hearted. I could never do something like that."

"Sure you could," Kate says. "You just haven't been desperate enough yet. Besides, women have been marrying men for money for millennia. If it's not broke don't fix it."

"I liked the old Kate better," mutters Arya. "At least when she dated the professional jet-skier, or that stand-up comedian, or the tennis instructor, she thought she was in love."

Kate sniffs. "I've grown up."

"More like regressed," Arya says.

"You're all forgetting something," Renee interrupts.

"What's that?"

Renee shakes her head. "You have to get the uptight bore to fall in love. That's the only reason a man would lose his head enough to marry these days. He has to be crazy in love. Trust me, I love my work too much, I'll never get married. From what I hear, Declan Fox feels the same."

I think back to our night on the island. I don't think Renee's right. In fact, I think Declan is a romantic underneath his stiff exterior. Unfortunately, he's also a thief and a relationship ruiner.

"Crazy in love is not a problem. Have you seen this?" Kate asks. She gestures to her face and her body.

Renee snorts.

But Arya, science-loving, calm, sweet Arya scowls, marches over to Kate and says, "Stop being a mercenary hag. Boobies mate for life, did you know that? And you can't even contemplate a year. You're being disgusting." Then she slaps her paint roller against Kate's chest.

Arya's roller hits Kate's breasts with a wet thwack. Kate gasps as Arya rolls coral paint all over her. Then Kate steps back and pulls her paint-soaked T-shirt away from her skin. She looks at Arya in shock.

"Did you just paint my breasts and call me a booby?"

Arya glares at her. "No. I called you a hag. You're worse than a booby. Your morals are lower than a booby's. You don't even compare. I'd never insult a booby by putting you on the same level."

Renee starts to laugh. "A moral booby."

Oh boy. This is not the time for Renee to start making booby jokes.

Kate and Arya both swing toward her.

"Stay out of it," they say at the same time.

Then Kate picks up her brush and flicks it so gobs of paint spray at Renee. The coral paint hits her black business suit and sprays droplets all over her pants and jacket.

"Hey!" shouts Renee. "I object."

But Kate's not done. She turns on Arya and slaps her paintbrush against Arya's cheek and wipes it over her face and down her neck.

I snort.

They all turn and look at me. A calculated gleam enters Kate's eyes, and I see it mirrored on Arya's and Renee's faces.

I hold up my hands in the universal surrender pose. "No way, guys. I'm an innocent party here. I have no opinion about boobies."

"But you have an opinion about Declan. And you think I shouldn't go after him, all based on hearsay," Kate says.

She bends over and dips her brush in the paint tray, soaking up as much paint as possible.

"That's not the definition of hearsay," Renee says. She grabs a roller from the tray and hefts it in her hand.

"Why are you gunning for me?" I ask Renee.

She shrugs. "Because it's fun."

"It's not. This is a painting party, not a people painting party." I take a step back.

Arya's roller squeaks as she moves it back and forth in the tray picking up more paint. "You should agree with me. Michael's lying, because Percy would never be friends with someone so awful."

"I do agree with you," I say. I take another step back. Paint is reallllly hard to get out of your hair.

"No you don't."

Okay. Fine. "You're right. I don't. Percy has bad taste in friends."

At that Arya jumps across the living room with her paint roller held out in front of her. I dodge her, but Renee anticipates my move. She slaps her paintbrush down my arm.

I shriek as the cold, thick paint slides over my skin.

Kate runs up and rubs paint over my face and in my hair. The smell of it fills my nose. "Gross, so gross."

I dodge away but Arya rubs her roller down my shirt and pants before I can get away.

"You're horrible. All of you are horrible." I'm laughing as I say this.

They're shrieking and whacking each other with paint. I

can't find a brush to fight back with so I dip my hands in the paint tray and coat them. Then I turn around and rush back into the paint fight. I rub my hands down Kate's cheeks, across Arya's arms, and all over Renee's formerly black business suit.

"Who's the booby now?" cries Kate.

"You'll never be a booby," Arya says. "Never."

I'm out of breath I'm laughing so hard. Every bare inch of my skin is covered in paint, and Arya and Kate aren't much better. Only Renee in her business suit has avoided paint-plastered skin. We all look like a coral-covered horror show.

"You guys, please. I surrender. Peace. Peace." My attempt to stop the madness is met with a paintbrush smacking the back of my head. The paint drips down my hair and then down my back.

I growl and turn around to confront of the culprit. "Kate...so help me."

She snorts. "You should see your face. You look so... so...disturbed!"

Ha. She's one to talk. Her hair sticks up in a blonde and coral mohawk and she looks like a toddler finger painted her.

"What's wrong with my face?" I ask in mock confusion. "I have a perfectly lovely face. Why is everyone always commenting on my face?" I stick out my tongue and cross my eyes. "Tell me I'm pretty Kate. Tell me."

"Noooo," says Kate. "I can't."

Renee starts to snicker. "You and Declan are the perfect match, Kate. Neither of you likes Isla's face."

"Tell me I'm pretty Kate," I say. I grab her shoulders and rub my face against her t-shirt. "Tell me."

It's too much. I burst out laughing.

Kate wipes her paint-covered hands on my face. "You're pretty, La-La. Of course you're pretty. I'd marry you tomorrow if you had a billion dollars. You'd be number one on my list. My parents would love you."

I grin at her. "That's better."

"Still not as good as a booby," Arya says.

"No one is," Renee says.

"Percy is," Kate says. "Right, Arya?"

"He invited me to visit England. He wants me to meet his parents," Arya says.

We all stop and stare at her in shock.

"Did he...did he propose?" I ask. Which I think is the question on everyone's mind.

Arya gives a shy smile. "He hinted at it."

Holy crap.

"Do you love him?" I ask.

"Who cares?" Kate says. "He'll have a title. He has a castle. Who cares if she loves him?"

Arya glares at Kate. "I do." Then she says, "I love him. I know it's crazy. But I do. I even threw out my fault-finding database. It doesn't matter with him."

I raise my eyebrows and the drying paint itches and stretches. If Arya threw out her database, then this is serious. More serious than I thought.

"That's it. He's the one," I say.

We're all silent for a minute as we let that settle in.

Then Kate says, "I talked a colleague into taking us on

a sunset sail tonight. I'll get Declan and Percy on board. It'll be the perfect spot for him to declare himself. You girls in?"

I scratch at the paint on my cheek. It falls off in little coral flakes. "I don't know..."

"You can bring Michael," Kate says.

"I'll come," Renee says. "I haven't been on a boat since my office Christmas party."

"If I bring Michael, it'll be awkward. I don't want things to be awkward."

"It's a sixty-foot sailing yacht," Kate says. "Besides, I'll keep Declan busy. He won't even notice you."

Hmmm.

There's a knock on the door. We all turn at the sound. I look at my friends. There isn't anyone who isn't completely covered in paint.

"Maybe they'll go away," Arya whispers.

The person knocks again.

And again.

"They aren't going away," Renee says.

I rub at my cheeks and more paint flakes fall off. Oh well. I walk to the front door and pull it open.

No one's there.

Instead, on the porch there's a package. It's a box, wrapped in brown paper with a gold bow. I take it inside.

"What is it?" Kate asks.

"I don't know." I set it down on one of the few clean spots left on the paint cloth on the floor.

"Who's it from?" she asks.

"I don't know," I say.

"Ooooh, a secret admirer," Kate says.

"Or a bomb," Renee says.

"Shhh," Arya says. "Let her open it."

I kneel down and unfold the bow, then unwrap the paper. The box is white cardboard. There aren't any markings. I pull off the lid. Kate, Arya and Renee have gathered behind me.

Inside the box is gold tissue paper. And sitting on the tissue paper is the turtle statue from the gala.

"Wow. That's...a turtle," Kate says. She sounds disappointed. I look over my shoulder and grin at her.

"I bid on it last night at the gala. I guess I won."

But then I frown, because honestly, my bid wasn't that high. I didn't actually think it was possible that I'd win.

"There's a card," Renee says.

She points out a small white envelope stuck to the side of the box.

I grab it and open it up. Inside is a small piece of paper. It says, "Look. A turtle. It's pretty, but you're even prettier."

I frown.

"What does it say?" Arya asks.

"It says I'm pretty," I say and I can hear the confusion in my voice.

"Who's it from?" Kate asks.

I look at the handwriting. It's bold, neat, the letters are in all caps. But there's no signature.

"It doesn't say." I bite my lip, then I smile. "But Michael was there when I bid on it. He said almost the same thing to me last night. That the turtle was beautiful, but I was more so."

"Awwww," Kate says. "He's sweet. It's a sign. You have to invite him for the sail."

I look back at my friends. They all seem to be in agreement. Well, except Renee, I don't think she cares. She's picking at the paint stuck beneath her nails.

"Fine," I say. "On one condition."

"What's that?"

"You hags help me clean up and actually paint these walls like you said you would."

Kate snorts and pulls me, Arya and Renee in for a hug. "Of course we will."

"This is going to be great," Arya says. "Just think, a romantic sunset sail. Thanks Kate. You're the best."

"I'm forgiven? You'll come to my wedding?" Kate asks.

Arya rolls her eyes. "You're not as mercenary as you're pretending to be."

"I know," Kate says. "But I do want to see my family."

"We'll be your family," I say.

With that, we get back to painting. After all, we only have a few hours before we need to scrub layers of dried paint off our skin and out of our hair so that we can look halfway decent for our sunset sail.

Arya is hoping for a proposal.

Kate is hoping for a ticket to England.

And I...I'd like to thank Michael for the gift.

I'll avoid Declan. But that goes without saying.

11

KATE IS RIGHT. SUNSET SAILS ARE THE PERFECT PLACE TO bring about all those romantic feelings.

I lean over the bronze railing and look down into the clear blue water. We're passing over a coral reef on our way to a nearby sandbar. A school of fish darts beneath the boat. The breeze ruffles my hair and sends the tendrils blowing across my face.

"What do you think?" I ask Michael.

He leans his forearms on the railing next to me. He's wearing a white shirt with his sleeves rolled up and khaki shorts. "To be honest, I'm surprised you invited me."

I hold onto the railing as the boat leans with the wind and moves us swiftly over the water. "Why? Of course I'd invite you. After the turtle and all..." I give him a smile. "I meant to say thank you."

"I enjoyed last night too." He smiles at me and I note

the freckles coming out on his face from being in the full sun for a day.

Michael looks around the sailboat. We're at the aft, near the wooden swimming platform. Kate and Declan are at the bow, facing forward into the wind. Kate's long blonde hair is tied up in a ponytail, and she's wearing a string bikini.

It's still an hour from sunset, so it's bright enough for the sun to sparkle over her and paint her in her best light. Declan's chin tilts up and I see his shoulders move as he takes a deep breath of the sea air.

I'm not certain how she convinced him to come. Probably Percy jumped at the chance and Declan felt obliged to come along to watch over his friend.

"I actually meant, I'm surprised you wanted to see more of me, since Dec seems to be a favorite of your friend's."

I shrug. "I'm not easily swayed by apparent status or wealth. I look to a person's character first."

"Admirable," he says. Then he glances at my ruffled bikini top and cut -off shorts, and with a humorous glint in his eye he says, "Admirable and beautiful. If I'd known Mariposa was so blessed, I'd have traveled here sooner."

I look away from him for a moment, trying to ignore the prickly feeling his compliment gives me. He's definitely not the subtle type.

When I turn back I ask, "Speaking of, why did you come to Mariposa? It's not the most popular destination."

A suspicion starts to niggle in the back of my mind. Did he follow Declan? Does he want to confront him?

Michael tilts his head and the wind ruffles his wavy hair. He studies me, then says slowly, "I know what you're thinking. But no. I didn't know Dec was here. I came for an entirely different purpose."

I tilt my sunglasses down my nose and say, "What? Long walks on the beach?"

He throws his head back and laughs, long and loud. When he does I notice Declan send an irritated glance our way.

I wave at him and give him a big toothy smile. He scowls and shakes his head then turns back to look out at the sea where Kate's pointing something out on the horizon.

"No, not long walks on the beach," Michael says, his voice full of mirth. "I came for an investment opportunity."

"Really? What kind of investment?"

Michael leans so close that I can smell the tangy scent of his cologne. "I can't say. Trade secrets and all that. But as soon as I heard about the opportunity I knew it would be profitable. I have high hopes."

Well, by his expression, he certainly seems sure that this investment will pan out.

"Wow," I say. "That sounds...vague."

He grins and his laugh lines deepen. He looks so happy that I can't help but smile back. He really is the friendliest guy.

"What business are you in? Am I allowed to know that?" I ask, my journalistic tendencies driving me to ask more questions.

He gives me a conspiratorial look and taps his nose twice. Apparently this is a secret.

"Mergers and acquisitions," he says. "I'm hoping to complete a profitable merger. There's a business here that suits my portfolio perfectly."

Wow. That's...unexpected.

"Ah. Well. I wish you luck."

At that he glances back to the bow of the boat. Perhaps he's worried that Declan will try to sabotage him again.

I frown. I hope that he won't, but what do I know?

Kate's no longer at the front of the boat. It looks like she went below to join Percy, Arya and Renee. There's a kitchen, couches, a bathroom, and a few bedrooms. This sailing yacht really is luxurious. Kate's colleague Rick and his wife Pilar own the boat. Pilar's below helping make dinner and Rick's at the helm.

"How about I go below and grab us some drinks?" Michael asks.

I look toward the bow at Declan. He's all alone, staring across the water.

"That sounds great," I say. "Thank you."

Michael holds the rail as he makes his way to the stairs. Once he's below I decide to head to the bathing platform at the end of the boat and get a closer look at the water.

The sun is closer to the sea. I love this time of day. The sun always paints the water in flames of gold that flicker with the waves, and stripes of orange and glossy apple red. Sometimes if you jump into the sea at sunset it feels like you're bathing in a rainbow. Flaming red, blueberry blue, grass green, canary yellow, tangerine. All you have to do is dive in and you're swallowed by a prism of color.

I crouch down on the wooden platform and lean forward to trail my hand through the sun-tinted water speeding past.

"I'd be careful if I were you."

Declan.

I stiffen. We haven't spoken since our night together. Or since I learned that he's an awful person.

"Isla," he says in a commanding tone. Probably the same one he uses at work to order his minions around.

Ugh.

I don't need him to tell me to be careful. I've been sailing since before I could walk. I know how to get around a boat.

I'm crouched down to reach the water, but crouching isn't the best way to scold Declan, so I quickly stand and spin around.

"Listen here. I'll have you know—"

I hit a puddle of water and my foot slips out from under me. I reach forward trying to grab a railing but there aren't any holds on the platform. Just open air. My arms spin in front of me. As I plunge backwards toward the water my eyes connect with Declan's.

He doesn't look stiff and pompous.

Nope.

The last thing I see before I hit the water is his shocked expression.

I hold my breath and kick for the surface. I have my eyes open, the water is clear, and there's still enough light to see the small reef below me. There's a Nassau grouper just beneath me and a school of silvery bar jack. A needlefish darts by.

My jean shorts drag against the water and my canvas shoes are heavy.

Then, I see something that surprises me.

Declan.

He's dived into the water.

I kick harder for the surface. He's underwater, his form is perfect, and he's kicking toward me, his eyes open.

I break the surface of the water and take a breath. A moment later Declan swims up next to me.

"Are you alright?" he asks. He wipes the water from his face and looks at me with concern. "Isla?"

I tread water and think about kicking off my shoes. Or kicking Declan.

"Isla? Are you alright?"

"Did you call out? Alert Rick before you jumped?" I ask tersely.

He stares at me, apparently trying to work out my question.

"I'm fine, I can swim," I say. "Did you shout out? You know, something like 'man overboard!' Did you alert anyone?"

I look past him at the sailboat. It's moving fast, my stomach drops when I realize it's already twenty meters away. I can't see Rick at the helm, which means he can't see me.

Declan's brow furrows. And I watch as the importance of what I'm saying slowly sinks in.

"No one knows we're out here."

"Right," I say.

"They don't know to turn around."

"Exactly," I say.

"They couldn't see the platform from the deck. They won't realize we're overboard until—"

"Until someone looks for us and realizes we're gone."

He stares at me.

I tread water, keeping my head above the surface.

"Do you think they'll...?"

I shake my head no.

"But will they..."

I keep shaking my head.

"You really wanted to spend another night with me, didn't you?"

He frowns at my ill-timed joke.

"In the sea? No."

As we stare at each other, the sailboat glides farther away, and the sun dips below the water.

It's night, and once again, we're alone together.

12

THE SAILBOAT HAS LONG SINCE DISAPPEARED AROUND THE eastern tip of the island. By mutual agreement, Declan and I stayed in the general vicinity of where we went overboard for a good fifteen minutes, but the boat hasn't turned back. Unfortunately, no fishermen or other boats have happened by.

In the evening, you can see Venus and Mercury near the horizon. The two planets look like large, brightly shining stars. Once it's dark enough, the real stars start to appear.

It's dark enough now. There are stars popping into view in the indigo blue sky. The water has shifted from translucent blue to opaque metal gray. I shiver and my teeth chatter a bit.

I'm cold now that the sun is down and the wind has picked up. But also, I hate not being able to see what's swimming in the water with me.

There could be barracuda, jellyfish, lionfish, sharks. I stop my mind from going down that path. If I start thinking about everything that could eat, maim, or menace us in the water at night, I'll not be fit to swim to shore.

"They aren't coming," I say. I swim a lot, but my arms are getting tired from treading in place.

"No," Declan says. It's just one word, but I think I can hear self-recrimination in his voice.

"Don't worry about it. I think it's time to swim back. It's only three thousand meters or so. If we keep Venus in front of us, we'll hit Bartlett Bay. Then we can walk to my place and call Kate. Let them know we're okay. You can swim that far?"

Three thousand meters isn't quite two miles. A fit swimmer can manage that in open water in less than an hour. A not so fit swimmer...well, I'm hoping Declan's a good swimmer.

"I'll be fine," he says in a tight voice.

I don't question him. Luckily, we're on the north side of the island, in the wide bay where the water is shallow-ish and calm. There aren't any rip currents or other hazards to be concerned about. Except, you know, the sea creature variety. I try not to think about sharks.

Arrgh. Planes and sharks. My two fears.

"Which one is Venus?" Declan asks.

"It's the brightest body in the sky, that one that looks like a star, near the horizon. It's to the south. Do you see it?"

"Alright," he says.

"We'll keep each other in sight," I say. "Stay next to me."

"Are you worried about me?" he asks, and there's a smile in his voice.

"Not at all," I lie. "Why would I be worried? It's not as if I like you or that I'm interested in you. In fact, if we hadn't both ended up in the water, I may have pushed you off the boat from sheer dislike."

He makes a disbelieving noise.

"Stay close," I say. "I'll be extremely upset if I have to save you." I try not to let any worry leak through into my voice.

"You're strange," he says.

Tell me about it.

I'm about to start swimming, when suddenly, a cold, slippery *thing* slams against my calf. I shriek and kick out.

"Shark! Shark!"

I take quick strokes and try to swim away from the shark I'm sure is circling.

"Isla," Declan calls.

"There's a shark," I call. I spit the sea water out of my mouth that I pulled in when I shrieked. "It hit me in the leg. It's testing to see if I'm good to eat."

Oh no. Oh no. I hate sharks.

"Isla. That wasn't a shark."

"How do you know? You're not from here. Come on. We have to swim."

Oh jeez. Oh no. I'm going to be eaten by a shark with Declan Fox. Then we'll both end up in its belly, mixed together, a tasty shark appetizer of limbs and organs and ack.

I start to swim.

"Hurry," I shout over my shoulder.

I kick my feet and do a quick crawl. I look back to make sure Declan's coming. I'm moving at a fast pace. Thankfully, Declan seems to be a pretty good swimmer. He has short strokes that chop at the water and he easily keeps pace with me.

After five minutes of my frantically paced swim, I slow down. I'm breathing hard, my heart thuds against my chest, and I feel like I'm going to throw up. It's either from my fear of sharks swimming below me unseen in the opaque water, or because I swallowed a few mouthfuls of sea water. Take your pick.

Declan slows his stroke and we pull close together, swimming with our heads above the waves.

"I think it's gone," I say. I haven't felt the shark bump me since the first time.

Declan looks over at me. The moon rose while we were swimming and its light reflects off the surface and paints his face in silvery color.

"Isla. There was no shark," he says. His voice has a tinge of humor. I'm not used to there being humor in his voice, so it takes me aback. Especially because I think he's laughing at me.

"How do you know?" I ask. "I felt it hit me. That's what sharks do. And there are plenty of sharks here. Nurse sharks, reef sharks, lemon sharks, hammerhead sharks—"

"It was me," he says.

I stop my recitation of all the sharks in the local waters. "What?"

"I'm sorry. I accidentally kicked you when I was treading water. It was me."

"You...you..."

I had been cold, but embarrassed heat rushes over me at the realization that I just swam like my life depended on it, because of a *foot*.

"You...weren't a shark."

If I weren't swimming, I'd smack my forehead. But maybe not, I'm too relieved. My heartbeat slows and the feeling of nausea fades.

I grin at Venus floating in the sky ahead of us. "It wasn't a shark."

"If you like, we can call it a foot shark," he says.

I scoff. "Stop joking around and swim. Like I said, I'm not in the mood to rescue you."

He laughs, and the low, gravelly sound makes my stomach clench.

We've made farther into the bay, where the water is calm and shallow, although not shallow enough to touch bottom. The taste of salt lingers on my tongue. My lips are cold, but if we keep moving I'll stay warm enough.

"Not that I'm making excuses," I say, "but I don't like the dark."

He reaches a hand up out of the water and tugs on a lock of my hair.

"I know," he says.

My stomach clenches again. The intimacy of that

gesture shocks me so much that I have nothing to say in response.

We keep swimming toward the beach at Bartlett Bay, the sound of our strokes splashing in the water. The moonlight flows across the water like a waterfall. It seems like it should be making a noise too. But it doesn't.

After a few minutes we start to swim freestyle again. We move quickly through the water. Declan swims next to me and we settle into a rhythm. Stroke, stroke, breathe, stroke, stroke, breathe. Check that he's still close. Stroke, stroke, breathe. It's almost like when we were paddling the kayak. I stay close to him, he stays close to me, and we move in the same direction, with the same cadence.

Time speeds by, moving past us like the water running over our skin. The only reason I know nearly an hour has passed is the crescent moon rising higher and Venus dimming and sinking lower. And because of my arms and legs, even though I'm in buoyant salt water, they feel heavy and fatigued. I can make out the dark outline of the palms and pines on the shore of Bartlett Bay only a few hundred meters away.

I reach out and touch Declan's shoulder. He slows and lifts his head.

"We're almost there. You still okay?" I ask.

"Never better," he says.

"Ha."

We start to swim toward shore again. But this time, instead of doing the freestyle, I keep my head above water and do a modified breaststroke. I can't see below the surface of the gunmetal gray and black sea, but I think

Declan is doing the same. He tilts his head to me and the moonlight drags across his face. His eyes glint in the light.

"Did you know?" he begins, then he stops.

"What?" I ask, curious as to what could make him stop mid-sentence.

"I've never had a gold digger go to such lengths to entrap me," he finally says. I quickly look over at him and the moonlight shows the smirk on his face.

I scoff, "You're the one who jumped in after me." I splash water at him and he chuckles, and his laugh is as opaque and unreadable as the ocean water.

"I didn't ask for you to spend another night with me," I say, just to make it clear where we stand.

"Noted," he says.

Then, I gasp. Because the water lights up. Literally lights up. Everywhere I touch, neon blue lights spark through the water. Declan is surrounded by ripples and waves of electric blue dancing across his skin and in the water around him.

"It's the bay," I say excitedly. Then I realize that doesn't make sense. "The bay is bioluminescent and these little microorganisms light up and...isn't it beautiful?"

Declan looks at me, then down at the aura of electric blue surrounding me. I'm treading water again, and it looks like I have trailing blue angel's wings.

"I never come out here," I say. "I mean, when I was a kid, my mom brought me. I thought the lights were fairies and that they were going to pull me underwater to live in their kingdom. I used to dream about it."

I glance over at Declan to see if he's laughing at me.

He's not, he's watching me with that same, neutral, stoic expression. I pull my hand through the water and watch the trail of blue sparks flash and pulse everywhere I touch. I imagine the lights as little fairies flying around my fingers. I look back at Declan. He's not watching the water, he's watching me. I lick my lips nervously. They taste of salt and the sea.

"My dad finally told me they weren't fairies, they were Pyrodinium Bahamanse, a microorganism. After that, I didn't ever feel like coming back."

I stop and look at the blue lights shining around Declan.

"Why not?"

Now that he asks, I'm not really sure. I swim closer to him.

"I'm not really sure," I admit. "I used to think it was because the magic was gone once my dad told me the science behind the lights. But now..." I look around at the bioluminescence. "I see that's wrong. It's still magical, even though I know there's a scientific explanation. It's still magic."

He doesn't say anything. Instead, he turns over and floats on his back, spreading his arms and legs so that he looks like a glowing blue angel floating in the water.

Then, he turns his head toward me and says, "Come on then."

I let out a surprised huff. "Alright," I say. "But it's not because I'm interested. It's only because it's magical." Then I spread my arms and legs out and float on my back.

The moon spills silvery light over us, and from the

corner of my eyes I can see the field of blue fairy lights sparking in and out of existence around us. It feels like we're floating in the middle of the deep, black universe and stars and planets are being born in brilliant blue flashes and then fading quietly away, only to be born again. And again.

The night is quiet. Neither Declan nor I speak. We just float together in bioluminescence. My arms extend out and I startle when my hand brushes against his.

He doesn't say anything, and neither do I.

Instead of pulling away, I leave my hand next to his. It's sort of lonely in a universe of floating blue lights, and it feels comfortable to have his hand close enough to hold, even if I never actually do reach out and take it.

He doesn't pull away either. So we float there, staring up at the crescent moon, a minute, two, five passing by. Touching, but not.

Finally, the draw of the bioluminescence fades and I remember that Kate and Arya and everyone else are probably frantic, that they've likely mobilized the coast guard.

"We need to go," I say. "We have to call and let them know we're okay."

"Right. Of course," Declan says. He flips over. The lights stir up as he starts to swim toward shore. I quickly follow after him, leaving the magic behind.

In less than five minutes we've made it to the beach. I stand on the shore in an ankle-deep pile of sargassum and my legs feel heavy and jellylike.

Declan stands up straight and stretches his arms

behind his back. His shoulders are stiff, and the closed expression on his face reminds me of the look he had after we spent the night together on the little island.

I take a breath of the sulfur scent of the sargassum and cough it back out.

"Come on, my place is this way," I say.

I expect now, after we make it to my cottage, Declan will return to his usual behavior. That stand-offish, rude, closed off man I don't understand.

It makes me cranky just thinking about it.

I start to jog up the beach path. Bartlett Bay has a public beach with a few picnic tables, benches and a bathroom. Just up the long, sandy path is the road that leads to my cottage. It's less than a mile away.

There's a slight breeze, and because my shorts and T-shirt are wet and clinging, I shiver. So, even though my legs feel like a jellyfish squishing across dry land, I jog faster, trying to keep warm.

Annoyingly, Declan doesn't have any problem keeping pace. In fact, I think he could easily run faster.

"Your boringly normal house is near here?" he asks.

I glance over at him, surprised that he remembers my description of it.

"Just up the hill," I say, ignoring the fact that I'm short of breath. Swimmer I am, runner I am not.

He gives a short grunt, apparently understanding that I'm not able to talk and run. We're quiet for the rest of the way. My feet are bare and the concrete, sand, and rocks scrape at the bottom of my feet. I'm embarrassed that I'm barefoot, I hate that I kicked off my shoes in the water. It's appalling how often flip flops and shoes wash up on our shores. But I couldn't swim nearly two miles with them on. As penance, I'll take a trash bag and do a beach cleanup this weekend.

Somehow, Declan managed to keep his on. Every step sends a squishy, squelching noise up to match the slapping of my bare feet on the pavement.

A few cars pass us, their lights shine over us, and some honk hello, but no one stops. Not that I flag them down. We're only a few minutes from my cottage.

My porch light is on. It shines bright in the dark night, a beacon on the hill over Bartlett Bay. I'm one of the few houses in the area.

"Just up there," I say.

I point to the top of the hill. I turn up the narrow, curving road, and Declan follows. I look at him from the corner of my eyes, to see if he's showing any emotion now that he's spied my "boringly normal" cottage, but he doesn't look any different than usual.

I'm glad to see it. A warm feeling courses through me when I see my porch light filtering through the sea grape leaves and the wispy pines. It's like that happy, expectant feeling you get when you see someone you love after they've been away for a long time. I get it every time I come home. Which, I suppose, is why it's home.

At my porch I open the front door and hold it wide for Declan.

"Come in. The bath is down the hall on the right. Grab a towel. I'm going to call Kate."

Declan nods. "Thanks."

I don't wait to see if he looks around. I hurry to the kitchen to the landline. Some people only have a cell here, but service is spotty, so I keep a landline too.

I punch in Kate's number. She answers on the first ring.

"Kate, it's me."

"La-La?" Then she yells, "It's Isla, everyone, it's Isla." Then, "Where are you? Is Declan there? Are you okay? What happened? La-La, what in the world? Why did you do that? I was so worried—" She cuts off and starts to cry, great big, hiccupping tears and I can't make out what she's saying anymore.

"I'm sorry," I say. "I'm at home. Declan's here. We're alright."

Kate's still crying. It seems she can't stop. Her stiff upper lip has failed her. I hear rustling, like the phone is being passed off.

"Isla, it's Renee," she has her lawyer voice on. "What happened?"

I cringe. "I fell off the boat. Declan jumped in after me."

There's silence on the other end. So I say, "We waited for the boat to come back, but when it didn't we swam to shore. I'm home now. We're both fine. I'm sorry for the trouble. Was the coastguard notified?"

They were.

A full search was in progress. Helicopters, search and rescue boats, the works.

"I'll notify them," Renee says. "I'll take care of it."

There's another rustling. "You're alright?" It's Arya.

"Hey. We're fine." In fact, I'm starting to feel incredibly embarrassed. "I'm sorry for all the trouble."

"Percy wants to know if Declan is okay," she says.

"He's fine. We're both fine."

After that, I make my excuses. I'm tired and drained and embarrassed at how many people went out of their way to find Declan and me.

I hang up the phone, wrap my arms around myself, and lean my head against a kitchen cabinet. I close my eyes and let out a long sigh.

I hear Declan's footsteps stop at the entry to the kitchen, but I don't turn around.

I'm beat.

"They all know we're alive," I say. "My friends are ecstatic. Not surprisingly, your friends and family are terribly sad you were found. They were hoping for an early inheritance."

I peek back at him and give him my best sassy smile, trying to lighten my mood. His expression doesn't change from that flat, neutral look he's so fond of.

"Shame," he says. "I so hate to disappoint."

"Hmm. Really?"

He crosses his arms over his chest. "No."

I grin big enough for the both of us. "I didn't think so."

When he doesn't smile back my skin starts to itch. Although, most likely that's the drying salt water, my sweat and my damp clothing.

Declan is still in his wet clothes, although I can tell he's toweled off. I imagine he's itchy and uncomfortable too.

I clear my throat. The kitchen feels smaller than it's

ever felt before. I can't imagine how it would feel if Declan stepped all the way inside. It's hard to remember how awful he is when I'm standing next to my grandma's sunny lemon-yellow countertops and the wood cabinets my grandpa made. The low hum of the refrigerator fills the silence and I can smell the ripe mangoes in the fruit bowl. I want to invite him to sit down at the table. I could make us dinner and a cup of hot tea.

Except, I keep forgetting, he stole an old man's pension, didn't he? He tried to ruin Michael's life. He did ruin Michael's relationship.

Declan Fox isn't a nice guy.

But that thought doesn't ring exactly true.

So I ask him, head on, "Are you a nice guy?"

He looks at me like I'm funny in the head.

Then without any hesitation he says, "No."

Right. "I didn't think so," I say.

His eyes flicker to the lemon-yellow countertops and something intangible passes over his expression.

"Do you like them?" I ask.

"Like what?"

"The countertops." I rest my hand on top of the cool, smooth laminate.

"Not particularly," he says.

I can't tell whether he's serious or not. So I choose not.

I shiver, I'm getting colder and itchier the longer I stay in my wet clothes. I really should kick Declan out. Let him fend for himself. Except, even if he isn't a nice person, I am. There aren't any taxis this far out of town and my car is at the harbor where the sailboat left from.

Even if we call a taxi, it'll be at least an hour until it arrives.

Before I head to the bathroom to dry off, and then to my bedroom to find a change of clothes, I have to ask something.

"Question," I say.

He nods.

"If you had a friend, and they were in love with someone who you believed wasn't right for them, would you try to prevent the match?"

He studies my expression carefully, like he's weighing his answer.

Then he says, "I'd do everything in my power to prevent it." He says this with more conviction than I've ever heard him use.

Goosebumps rise on my skin. There's my answer.

"Even if it's not your place? None of your business?"

He frowns at me like he's surprised I have the gall to question him.

I shake my head. Enough. I point to the first cupboard on the wall.

"Tea's on the bottom shelf. Kettle's on the counter. I'll be back in a moment. I'll make dinner, then you can go."

His presence is too much. Too large for my little cottage. Plus, he's admitted that he's not nice, that he's awful.

Not that I didn't already know that.

I walk past him, careful not to brush against him as I squeeze past, my legs still feeling like jelly.

13

I HAVE A QUICK RINSE IN A STEAMING HOT SHOWER, scrubbing off the salt and the sand.

In my bedroom I pull on a pair of cotton shorts and a Save the Turtles tank top and put my wet hair in a bun on top of my head. I look at myself in the mirror. No makeup, no cute dress, no styled hair. It's just me, looking like I do when I'm lounging at home or going to bed.

What does it matter? It's not as if I'm trying to impress Declan.

Five minutes has passed since I left him in the kitchen. I step around my queen bed and open my closet door. I shove aside a dozen dresses and pull out a large cardboard box. I kneel next to it and open the flaps.

A little cloud of dust floats up and hangs in the air for a moment. There's a peculiar feeling itching over my skin. I rinsed all the salt water off, so the itch must be because this is the first time I've opened this box since Theo and I broke up three years ago. He left the island shortly after we broke up and I never had the heart to throw his things away.

There are his reggae vinyl records, his snorkel and fins, his toothbrush, his favorite brand of sunscreen, a Rubik's cube he swore he'd finish someday, and a few pairs of shorts and T-shirts. All the clothing is folded neatly and everything else is stacked in a precise row.

Looking at it makes me uncomfortable. I remember the exact day I put all this away. It was a month after Theo left, and I still thought that he might come back. I never opened it again, but now I see, that lonely hope was still there, hidden, but waiting.

I shake my head at myself and wipe my hand over my face. Putting the maudlin aside.

I grab the T-shirt and pair of shorts on top of the pile and kick the box back into the back of the closet.

Then there's a loud bang. I jump.

"What the...?"

Bang.

There it is again. And again. It's a rhythmic thud and banging noise. It sounds like a...hammer?

I put the clothes under my arm and hurry down the hall.

When I come out in the living room, sure enough, there's Declan with a hammer. His back's to me. He has my toolkit at his feet and my hammer in his hand. He pulls the hammer back and thwacks the molding around my grandpa's built-in bookshelves.

"What are you doing?" I say.

He swings around quickly. There's a look of surprise on his face, although I'm not sure why he's surprised since he's whacking my wall with a hammer and making enough noise to wake the whole hilltop.

I point at the hammer in his hand. "Why do you have my hammer?"

He looks down at the hammer like he's actually surprised that he's holding it. Then he looks back up at me and there's such a guilty expression on his face that I almost start to laugh.

"The molding was loose. It was tilted a centimeter to the right," he says stiffly, as if this is a perfect explanation as to why he pulled out my toolbox and started hammering away.

"So, you thought it best to what? Find my toolbox in the hall closet and start hammering nails?" I lift my eyebrows.

He blinks at me slowly and I'm not sure that he heard what I said. Mainly because he's staring at my Save the Turtles tank top and cotton shorts. He has a funny look on his face.

That's when I realize that maybe *not* trying to impress Declan was the wrong move. Because my tank top is loose and sometimes flashes the edges and tops of my breasts, and my cotton shorts are so worn as to be almost see-through.

Right.

I clear my throat and Declan shakes his head and quickly looks back at my face. I've never seen him so uncomfortable.

He carefully sets the hammer on the nearest open space in the bookshelf.

"Careful of the turtle," I say quickly.

The glass turtle that Michael got me is right next to the head of the hammer. Declan's eyes flicker back to mine, his mouth forms an almost smile and he nods at me.

"I thought your grandpa would want his shelves to be straight. I apologize for the presumption," he says.

It's my turn to feel uncomfortable. That's actually... really nice.

For lack of anything better to say, I tell him, "Thank you."

Then I hold out the clothing in front of me. They're sort of like a shield so that I don't have to feel this basket-full of confusion I get handed whenever I'm around Declan.

"You can grab a quick shower and change into these. They should fit." I thrust the shorts and T-shirt at him.

He takes them and when he does his hand brushes over mine. My eyes widen. What the heck? I try to swallow but my throat is too dry.

"Your boyfriend's?" he asks.

"Ex," I say. "Three years, ex."

His expression doesn't change, so I'm not sure why I felt the need to clarify.

The silence is thick and the newly painted coral walls seem too bold and bright.

Declan makes the first move. He steps around me, toward the hall.

"Thank you," he says. I stare at the newly fixed

molding and listen to his footsteps walk across my squeaky, old, wood-planked floor.

He pauses. "Isla?"

I don't turn around. "Yes?" I hold my breath. My eyes widen and I try to keep my shoulders relaxed and my hands unclenched.

"The tea is ready."

I blow out my breath and close my eyes. "Okay. Thanks."

Jeez. *Jeez.*

What is *wrong* with me?

I shake my head and castigate myself. It's Declan. The jerky, toady, not-a-nice-man, pension-stealing, relationship-ruining, she's-not-good-enough-for-me Declan Fox.

"Idiot," I mumble.

"Isla?"

My eyes fly open. Declan's still behind me. He didn't leave. My cheeks burn, but I don't turn around.

"Yes?" I drawl slowly.

"Your shorts are see-through. I can see your...bananas."

What? Oh my gosh. No. Noooo.

I drop my hands to cover my bum. Then, I swing around quickly, my cheeks flaming.

I'm about to yell at him, but he's already down the hall, closing the door to the bathroom.

"Jerk," I hiss. "Idiot. Gah."

Why did I have to wear my hot pink and yellow dancing bananas underwear? Why? Why, Isla, why? And why did I have to wear my oldest, rattiest lounge clothes?

Was it to make a point, or was it my subconscious wanting to show Declan my banana-assets?

The pipes groan as Declan turns on the shower and then I hear the rush of water hitting my old porcelain bathtub.

I shake out of my mortification and rush to my bedroom. I strip out of my tank top and shorts and throw on a fuchsia wrap dress. Then I rush back to the kitchen, determined to get there, pour myself a cup of tea, calm my breathing, and act like nothing happened.

I hear the shower turn off while I'm pouring the amber-colored Earl Grey into my mug. I grab another mug from the cupboard and splash tea into it. The door to the bathroom closes and I hear Declan's steps coming down the hall toward the kitchen.

I let out a long breath and smooth my face into a look that I hope borders between unperturbed and amused. When I hear him enter the kitchen, I turn slowly with our mugs held in my hands.

I feel the amused look slip from my face.

He's in Theo's shorts and shirt, but he looks way better than Theo ever did. Way better.

I set the mugs down on the table with a hard thunk.

"Have some tea," I say.

Then I turn around so that I don't have to look at him in my ex's Mariposa half-marathon t-shirt and canvas shorts. Declan is broader and more muscular than Theo was, so the shirt fits him well. Too well.

I clatter around in the cupboards and pull down two

plates, two salad bowls, and then grab silverware. I'll set the table and make a quick meal. Then Declan can go.

Yes. Go. He needs to go.

When I turn back around, Declan is still standing in the entry, staring at me.

I look down at my dress then scowl back up at him.

"It's not because of what you said."

He shakes his head. "I didn't think it was."

"I don't care if you see my bananas."

He shrugs, "*I* don't care if *I* see your bananas."

I narrow my eyes, but he keeps his face neutral.

"Or my coconuts," I add, remembering the coconut conversation on the island.

"I'm not interested in coconuts," he says.

I drop the dishes to the table. "Perfect."

He folds his arms across his chest. "Wonderful."

We stare at each other for a moment, neither of us breaking eye contact. Then a slow smile spreads across my face, I can't help it.

"Stop smiling at me," he says.

I smile even harder. "Stop looking at me."

This time he does. He turns away and looks around the kitchen. My body loosens and I let out the breath I didn't realize I was holding.

Declan's eyes travel over the lemon-yellow countertops, the white cupboards, and the teal backsplash. Then he takes in the old appliances, the chandelier hanging from the ceiling and the plank floors. Funny enough, he's giving my kitchen a more careful looking over than he's ever given me. Even so, as his eyes drift over the room, it feels like they're drifting over me.

Goosebumps rise over my arms and I rub them.

"I'm going to make a quick dinner, then you can call a taxi."

Declan finally looks back at me, "That's not necessary."

"The taxi?"

"The meal."

I shrug. "Your loss. I picked up snapper at the fish market earlier today. It's been marinating in lime."

His mouth tightens and he frowns at me. I think I'm imagining it, but I swear his stomach growls.

"And I have coconut shrimp and Johnny cakes, that's a delicious deep-fried bread if you didn't know. And I made cassava cake yesterday..." I trail off, because Declan is staring at my mouth with the hungriest expression on his face. And now I'm not sure that it was such a good idea to try to convince him to stay.

"You don't have to stay," I say.

He shakes his head and pulls out the chair at the kitchen table. The legs make a scraping noise against the wood.

"I'll stay," he says.

"You really don't have to..."

I stop talking, and when he lifts an eyebrow at me I feel myself blush. Instead of continuing the conversation I go to the refrigerator and pull out all the ingredients. Then I heat the pans and start a deep fry pot for the Johnny cakes and coconut shrimp.

My grandma taught me to cook, and I move quickly

through the kitchen, chopping, and mixing and tossing ingredients into the pan.

I'm aware of Declan, sipping tea at the table, his eyes following my movements. After a while, the itch that his trailing eyes leave on my skin turns into a warm, glowing buzz. Sort of like the glowy feel the bioluminescence left on my skin.

Soon, the scent of fried dough, lime-marinated snapper, and shaved coconut fills the air. The snapping pop of the oil when the batter hits it, and the crackling of the fish in the pan fills the silence. It's a soothing sound that reminds me of weekends in the kitchen with my grandma and Sunday dinners with my family. A soothing, normal sound.

I plate the snapper, the shrimp, and the Johnny cake, then I throw freshly chopped vegetables into the salad bowls. I set the plates on the table and give Declan a small smile.

"Dinner, Mariposa style," I say.

His eyes flick from my face down to the plates. "Thank you."

I put the salad on the table and then grab pineapple water from the fridge.

"Bon appétit," I say.

Declan waits until I've taken the first bite, then he picks up his fork and tastes the snapper.

For some reason, I'm nervous. Cooking is such an intimate thing. I'd like to tell myself it isn't, but it is. I really shouldn't have invited him to stay, but he jumped in the water after me, he swam to shore with me, he...

"I still think you're awful," I say.

"This is really good," he says at the same time.

I purse my lips together and try not to react to his censorious look.

"Thank you. It's my grandma's recipes."

"Ah," he says.

We both start eating again. The snapper is flaky, the coconut shrimp has the perfect crunch, and the Johnny cakes are warm and chewy. I'm so hungry from the long swim that I stop thinking about Declan and just eat and eat until my plate is clean.

When I finish, I lick my fork one last time then look up. Declan's watching me. He's leaning back in his chair and his eyes are hooded. It looks like he finished eating a while ago.

"Had enough?" I ask, trying to cover my embarrassment at being completely and totally consumed by my meal.

He considers my question, and for some reason my mind fills with thoughts of what "had enough" could refer to. An image of us on the beach, Declan on top of me saying, "do I look like I've had enough?" flickers through my mind. I cough and start wheezing. Declan starts to stand but I wave him back and hit my chest.

"Fish bone," I say. "I'm fine." My voice is scratchy. I grab my glass of water and take a long gulp.

"Alright?"

"Fine," I say again. "Fine."

Then I stand up and clear the dishes. Declan brings the salad bowls to the sink. I can feel the heat of him behind me. I turn, and since my body is doing things that I don't like, I decide to remind myself of why Declan isn't right for me at all.

"Michael told me you and his dad were partners," I say.

He stiffens, and the warmth is sucked out of the room and replaced by the cold coming off Declan. By the look on his face this isn't a topic that he wants to discuss.

Oh well.

We don't always get what we want.

I don't want to be feeling like he and I are about to have a banana and coconut party in my pants.

"Why did you take his pension? How could you screw him over like that?" Bluntness, that's one of my most endearing qualities.

If possible, Declan's face becomes even more glacial. "Pardon?"

I'm no dummy, I can tell that his "pardon" is the polite way of saying "mind your own business."

But I can't. I don't understand how Declan can seem decent one second and then like the most awful jerk the next.

"You shouldn't take old people's pensions. It's despicable."

Declan's jaw tightens, which makes me notice how nice his jaw is, which really, really irritates me.

"We entered a partnership," he says stiffly. He drops the dishes into the sink and they clatter around.

"Partners don't ruin each other's lives," I say.

"I agree."

He steps back and stares at me. I shiver at the coldness on his face. It reminds me of the look he had at the gala.

"So, you're saying you made a mistake?"

"I made a terrible mistake."

"Oh." My righteous anger sort of fizzles out. "Then you should let him know." Or, at least, let Michael know.

I move past him and collect the rest of the dirty dishes and carry them to the sink. Then I remember something else.

"And on top of that, you should stop interfering in other people's relationships."

His forehead wrinkles. "Why would I do that?"

"Oh, I don't know. A thousand reasons. The first one being that it's horrible, second it's rude, third—"

I walk past him, but cut off when he reaches out and loosely grabs my hand. I stop, stunned at the intimate contact, and turn back around and look up at him. His hand is hot. His fingers squeeze mine, but he's holding me so loosely that I can pull away if I want.

"Third?" he says.

I blink at him. My mind feels as cloudy as the ocean on a turbid day. I can't remember what I was going to say. I lick my lips and try to breathe out the tightness in my chest.

"Just...stop..."

He lifts his eyebrows in question.

His hand clasping mine is doing funny things to my insides.

"Leave Percy and Arya be," I finish lamely.

He gives me a confused look. "Were we talking about Percy and Arya?"

I decide that we were. "Yes. Leave true love alone."

He raises his eyebrows and lets go of my hand. "Anything else?"

I clench my hand into a fist and try to make it forget the feel of his hand grasping mine.

"No," I say. Then, "Why were you holding my hand?"

For a second he looks uncomfortable. "I was swept away by the boring normalcy of your kitchen."

I snort. And I think he's almost, almost about to smile.

"You're confusing," I say.

"I'll do the dishes," he says at the same time.

So I let him. Because who doesn't jump at an offer like that? I sit at the table, drink tea, munch on leftover cassava cake, and watch him scrub my pots and pans.

"Why are you laughing?" he asks, looking over his shoulder. And I realize that a chuckle must've slipped out.

"I suppose it's because I've never had a billionaire wash my dishes before, and I expect I never will again. My grandma would've loved this."

His expression doesn't shift. "What about your parents?"

I shift on my seat and it creaks beneath me.

"Oh, you know. My dad wouldn't care because it doesn't involve bullets. My mom, I suppose she'd say you're displaying the traditional male mating behavior of..."

I stop talking. My eyes open wide and I clear my throat. Hard.

"I didn't mean...you're not actually..."

He lifts an eyebrow and I hear the silverware he's holding plunk back into the sudsy water in the sink.

"She's an anthropologist," I say. "She equates everything to mating rituals or rites of passage. I didn't mean you're actually—"

"Alright," he says.

"Okay."

"It's fine."

"Perfect," I say. Then I stand up and walk over to the phone. "I'll call a taxi."

"Thank you," he says.

After the call, when I sit down, the clanking sounds of Declan washing dishes are loud and uncomfortable in the silence.

When he's finished he pulls the plug on the sink and the water glugs down the drain.

He wipes his hands on the tea towel hanging from the cupboard and turns around to face me.

"Thank you," I say. I look down at the table. "And thank you for jumping in and swimming back with me." I glance up, "Even if it would've been better to get help onboard."

"You're welcome," he says, ignoring the last bit.

Then, because I can't leave this unsaid, I say, "I don't think you're awful anymore. You're only half awful."

I wait for his response, but he turns his face to the side and looks away from me. In the window's reflection I see a small smile curve at the edge of his lips.

Then the taxi pulls up the drive, the headlights shine through the window, and his reflection is wiped away.

"Well. That's the taxi. So. Thanks again."

He nods. "Anytime."

He starts to walk out of the kitchen but pauses at the hall and turns. "Isla?"

"Yes?" Annoyingly my heart beats a little faster.

"Thank you for dinner."

I nod. "You're welcome."

He studies me for a moment, then says, "I'm still not interested."

His words hit my warm, contentment like a glass of ice water. Gah.

"Oh, go away." I grab a clementine from the fruit bowl and chuck it at him.

He's too stunned to dodge. It hits him in the center of the chest then thuds to the ground.

He looks down at it then up at me. He scoffs. "Really?"

"Go on," I say. "You're back to awful. Full awful."

I grab for the squishy apricot at the top of the fruit pile and heft it in my hand.

He holds up his hands. "I surrender."

"I should've left you for the sharks," I say.

I throw the apricot at him, but this time he's ready. He snatches it from the air and holds it up for me to see.

"Goodnight Isla," he says.

I scowl at him.

Then he lifts the apricot to his mouth and takes a bite. The juice from the fruit runs over his lips and down his chin.

His tongue sweeps out and catches it up.

His eyes don't leave mine. Not the whole time he's licking up the juice of the apricot.

Oh my.

My abdomen clenches in response to the look on his face and my mouth starts to water.

"Goodnight, good riddance," I say, proud that my voice is steady.

"Goodbye, Isla."

He salutes me with the apricot and walks out of my cottage.

14

IT'S NOT QUITE SEVEN WHEN THE DOORBELL RINGS. THE morning light is only just penetrating my thick bedroom curtains. I groan at the insistent chiming.

"Go away," I manage to croak out. Then I grab a pillow and cover my head.

The doorbell chimes again.

"No," I mutter. I squeeze my eyes shut tight.

If I ignore them they'll go away. I didn't get to sleep until the early morning hours. Every time I closed my eyes I kept seeing Declan take a bite of that apricot. The juice would run down his lips, then he'd look at me, all hungry-like, and lick them.

It was horrible.

Mainly it was horrible because I don't think he actually had that ravenous, strip-you-out-of-your-pants look in his eyes when he bit the apricot in real life. That was purely a fantasy of my twisted imagination. Which unfortunately means my subconscious has decided that Declan is an *object of attraction* and I am the unwilling participant in my mind's fantasies.

So, every time I closed my eyes to sleep, my imagination took me on a train ride to Declan's lustful gaze. Therefore, I did the only thing a reasonable woman can do in the middle of a lust-fueled, sleepless night, I kept my eyes open and my mind occupied by watching a five-hour marathon of home renovation shows.

Except, every time a man picked up a hammer my stomach got all squishy and funny. So, the shows weren't that helpful either.

It may be morning, a fresh new day, with someone at the front door ready to chat, but I'm tired. Really tired.

The doorbell chimes again. And again.

I groan.

Whoever's here isn't going away.

My cellphone starts to ring.

I lift the pillow off my head and grab my phone from the nightstand. "'lo?" I mutter when I swipe to answer.

"Isla, open the door. We want coffee. And breakfast."

It's Arya. She sounds annoyingly chipper. I squeeze my eyes shut. They feel all gritty and bloodshot.

"Who's we?" I ask. My voice is all froggy and croaky.

"Me and Michael."

I scramble upright as soon as Arya mentions Michael.

Michael's here? On my doorstep? With Arya?

Suddenly, I feel guilty over my uncontrollable, undesired nighttime fantasies.

"What are you doing here?"

I jump out of bed and rush to my closet. I need to get dressed. In something cute and preferably non-see-through.

"We didn't come together," Arya says, unaware of my frantic shuffling through my closet. "He pulled in after me. We're both worried and wanted to see how you're doing. I have an hour before work. You can make your grandma's banana fritters and reassure us that you survived."

I pull a floral patterned dress over my head then pop the phone back to my ear.

"I'm alive," I say. "Couldn't I reassure you by going back to bed?"

"No," she says mulishly. "Let us in or I'll use the spare key."

"Give me two minutes."

I drop the phone and rush to the bathroom. Then I take thirty seconds to splash my face with cold water, finger comb my hair, and put on lip gloss.

When I pull open the door I put on a smile and pretend that I've been awake for at least an hour. To be fair, Arya knows I usually wake up around five, so that isn't a stretch.

"Morning," I say.

Arya beams at me. "Thank goodness. You *are* alive."

I hold the door open wide. "Come on in."

Michael looks fresh and well-rested. He has a sheepish smile on his face and is holding a bouquet of bright yellow Gerber daisies.

"I came to apologize. I'm terribly sorry I left you alone and that you fell overboard. If I had been there..."

If he'd been there I wouldn't have gone down to the platform and Declan wouldn't have approached me. We wouldn't have swum together, or seen the bioluminescence, or had dinner together.

And...I wouldn't have had a sleepless night blocking out images of apricots.

Instead, I would've had a casual, relaxed evening chatting with Michael while watching the sunset.

"Don't worry about it," I say. "I'm fine. Everything turned out alright."

He extends the flowers to me, and I take them. The paper wrapped around the flower stems crinkles in my hands.

"Still. I feel that I'm at fault. Please accept my apology."

I hold back a smile. I don't think my falling off the sailboat was connected to Michael in any way, but if he wants to buy me flowers then he's perfectly welcome to do so.

I lean down and breathe in their fragrance. Gerber daisies don't have much of a smell, it's light, nearly not there, but to me, the scent is like a summer day at the beach. Breezy and green.

"If it makes you feel better, I accept. Although, you didn't do anything wrong."

I smile at Michael and his sheepish look transforms into one of relief.

"Thank goodness. I was frightened that my only friend on the island would avoid me after yesterday."

"Definitely not," I say.

I clasp the flowers to my chest. It's been years since anyone has given me a bouquet.

"How about those banana fritters?" Arya asks. She nods her head toward the kitchen.

What a mooch.

I glare at her and subtly tilt my head toward Michael.

"I'll start the coffee," she says.

She turns and heads down the hallway toward the kitchen. My friends come over in the early morning often enough to know where the coffee beans and French press are.

Michael and I remain quiet until we hear Arya opening cupboards and pulling down mugs.

"Thank you for coming to check on me," I say.

I look Michael over. He really is cute in a down to earth, nice guy kind of way. His short walnut-brown hair is shiny and soft and has a bit of wave to it and his cheeks have a permanent pink tint to them. Like he's always happy or embarrassed. This morning he's dressed in linen pants and a white collared shirt. Business-like but casual.

He nods and puts his hands in his pockets. "Kate told me your address last night and suggested I stop by..." He clears his throat.

Apparently, Kate has decided that I should definitely hook up with Michael. She's completely transparent. I can imagine her grand plan. A triple summer wedding on the beach. Where Declan, Percy and Michael all wait at the altar for Arya, Kate and me to walk down the aisle.

I cringe at the thought.

In my imaginings, Declan punches Michael, then

Michael tackles Declan, and the entire arched wedding arbor collapses on top of them.

Guests scream and run down the beach.

Hungry seagulls swoop down and carry away the wedding cake.

Kate descends into tears and Arya catalogues how many birds come to steal our wedding favors.

It'd be chaos.

Absolute chaos.

Kate's out of her mind.

"That was nice of Kate," I say.

He nods, then looks at the flowers in my hand.

"I have a breakfast meeting on the other end of the island, but perhaps this weekend we might see each other? If it isn't an inconvenience to you? I'd like to make up for our interrupted evening."

He's so polite. Charming.

This is how a man should behave toward a woman.

I search for a spark, some bit of feeling that tells me Michael and I might travel further along the road to romance.

My stomach growls, and there's an empty gnawing feel in my gut. If I were being generous I might catalogue that as lustful enthusiasm, but honestly, I'm just hungry for fritters.

But that's alright. Like I told Declan, my ideal man is the one who is normal, average, who doesn't light my fire, until after months or years into our platonic relationship, he suddenly...does.

After we have dinner together, watch movies together,

fix up my house together, go to the beach. All those normal things. Laying the foundation for a relationship that lasts a lifetime.

"That sounds wonderful. We'll have dinner," I say, deciding that Michael will definitely, probably, maybe someday be *the one*.

"Until then," he says.

Then he touches his hand to his head in a sort of tipping his metaphorical hat salute and jauntily walks out the door.

Arya comes out of the kitchen.

"Coffee's ready," she says.

We both watch Michael drive away in his rented 4x4.

"I still think he's a rat," Arya says. And in case I didn't remember that rat is one of Arya's worst insults, she adds, "Rats steal nesting birds' eggs."

"Rats don't bring flowers," I say. I hold up the sunny yellow daisies.

She shrugs. "Percy doesn't trust him."

"Why? Did he say something specific?"

We walk toward the kitchen.

"No," she admits, "just that if Declan doesn't care for him then he must have a good reason."

I snort. "Declan doesn't care for anyone he meets, with or without a reason."

I block the image of the apricot that's trying to nudge its way into my mind.

We step into the kitchen and the smell of delicious coffee surrounds me. I feel more awake already.

"I guess swimming to shore with him didn't change your opinion."

I'm silent as I pour two mugs of coffee. I pull out a tin of sweetened condensed milk for Arya, open it and hand her a spoon. She drops two heaping tablespoons into her mug.

Finally, after a long sip of coffee, I say, "He probably isn't as awful as I thought, but he's not as nice as Percy believes either. I asked him about Michael's father, he admitted to taking the money, but he also said he's sorry."

"Huh." Arya looks nonplussed. "So he did take the money?"

I nod.

"Huh." Her nose wrinkles. "I suppose Percy doesn't know everything after all."

Then her eyes go all gaga in love, so I send her a cheeky grin. "We both know that I'm alive and well, but how about you? What did you and Percy get up to last night?"

She bounces in her seat and I can tell she's trying her best not clap her hands in excitement.

"He said he has something important to ask me. He was going to last night, but then you and Declan disappeared and we were all so worried but..." She sends me a happy, glowing look. "He told me he wants to see me tonight. To ask me something *important*."

"He's going to propose," I say, certain that *important* means proposal.

Arya swallows and then nods, repressing a smile. She's in her usual get-up: cargo pants, long-sleeve oxford shirt with the Department of the Environment logo and hiking boots, but she's looking especially beautiful today. I'd say it's love.

I wonder, if I ever fall into true love, if I'll be able to look at myself in the mirror and see such a noticeable difference in my appearance? Or will it only be obvious to my friends?

"This calls for banana fritters," I say.

"Huzzah!" Arya jokes.

I laugh and get busy frying up Arya's favorite breakfast. While I cook she details every moment of the previous night. How she and Percy had the most fascinating discussion about migration patterns, the nesting habits of cave swallows, and how he saved a sparrow with a broken wing when he was a boy.

When everyone discovered that Declan and I were missing, Percy and Renee took charge and notified the coastguard and mounted the search. In Arya's eyes, Percy is the perfect man, and I can't see anything to dissuade her.

"You're going to be very happy," I say.

She smiles as I set a plate of fritters on the table. The caramelized banana and sugar scent wafts up. My mouth waters in anticipation of the first sweet, crisp bite.

My doorbell rings.

Arya and I both look toward the front of the house.

"Who else?" I ask.

Not Declan. I flush. Maybe Declan. No, definitely not Declan.

"La-La, are you up?" Kate yells. Then, she hollers,

"Wake up!" Which, I think, woke every man, woman, child and creature on this side of the island.

Arya smirks at me.

"At least she waited until seven thirty," I say.

I hurry to the living room and pull open the front door. I gesture for her to come in. "Morning, sunshine. Arya's already here. There's banana fritter's on—"

"They're gone," she cuts me off.

Her nose is pink and her eyes are red rimmed. Has she been crying?

She isn't as put together and stylish as usual. In fact, she's without make-up, in sweatpants, flip flops and a tank top, and her hair is knotted and uncombed.

"Are you okay?" I ask. I'm shocked at her appearance.

She opens her eyes wide and pushes past me into the living room.

"Did you hear me? They're gone." She says this like she's announcing a hurricane hit the island while we were sleeping.

I shut the door behind her and follow her into the kitchen. Arya has already cleared a third of the fritters and has a fork halfway to her mouth.

"Err, morning, Kate. Want some?" she asks. Her mouth is full so it sounds more like errrmorning ate. Aant rum?

Kate gives her a look that seems to ask, *how can you be eating at a time like this?*

"They've left the island," Kate says.

Arya shrugs and pops the forkful of fritter into her mouth.

I grab another mug and pour Kate a cup of coffee. She looks like she could use it. I hand it to her.

"You should start from the beginning," I say.

Kate sets the coffee down on the kitchen table and lets out a long sigh. Her shoulders cave inward and I think she's trying to hold in tears.

"They left on the seven a.m. flight to Miami."

Oh. I have a feeling I know where this is going, but I'm not letting myself reach the logical conclusion. Arya puts down her fork and gives Kate her full attention.

"Who left?" she asks.

Kate winces. "Declan and Percy."

For a moment, Arya looks upset. She puts her hand on her stomach and I think maybe she regrets eating so many fritters. But then she brightens.

"Oh. Oh, that's so sweet." She smiles at me. "I bet he went on a day trip. Maybe he's going to pick up something special at a store in Miami."

An engagement ring goes unsaid.

"They'll catch the five o'clock flight back tonight," Arya says. She nods at me, reassured by her own logic.

I'm not so reassured. Kate wouldn't look like she does if they were coming back tonight.

"You don't understand," Kate says. She looks at Arya and then at me. The coffee in my empty stomach churns uncomfortably.

"Declan left a voicemail this morning. He and Percy have decided to leave the island. He won't be needing me as his realtor anymore because he won't be returning." Her lower lip wobbles.

"Won't be returning tonight?" Arya asks.

Kate shakes her head.

"Won't be returning this week?" she asks.

Kate gives her a level look. "Won't be returning ever."

"Ever, ever?" Arya asks.

Kate falls down into a kitchen chair and drops her head to the table. She knocks her forehead against the wood and moans, "My white whale"—*thump*, she knocks her forehead on the table again. "My ticket home"—*thump*—"gone"—*thump*—"my white whale's gooooone." *Thump.*

Arya stares at Kate, and I don't think what Kate's saying has sunk in.

Arya taps Kate's shoulder and she stops knocking her head against the table to look up.

"What? Can't you see I'm mourning the loss of my triumphant return home?"

"Pull it together," Arya says. She grabs a fritter and waves it in front of Kate's face. Kate takes a bite, brightens and then grabs the fritter to eat the rest.

When she's swallowed the entire thing, Arya asks, "Are you certain Percy left too?"

I can only imagine what Arya's thinking. If Percy has left, he isn't going to meet her tonight, and he certainly isn't going to ask her his important question.

"I'm certain," Kate says. "He specifically said, 'Mr. Oliver and I are leaving the island. We will not be returning. It doesn't suit our needs. Please discontinue the search for properties. That is all.'"

I cringe a bit at her cold recitation of his voicemail.

Unfortunately, I can easily imagine him saying something like that.

My chest feels a little achy and hollow.

He's left. And he didn't say goodbye.

Arya shakes her head. "That can't be true. Percy was taking me to dinner on the water tonight. He was going to ask me..."

Arya's face loses the happy glow it had.

"Can we hear the message?" I ask. Maybe Kate misunderstood.

She shrugs, pulls out her phone and plays the message on speaker. The message is from five this morning. Right around the time I finally fell asleep.

Declan's voice comes out loud and clear.

"Miss Collingwood. This is Declan Fox."

"I know who you are," mutters Kate unhappily.

I wrap my hands around my mug of coffee. His voice is so stiff and formal it makes me cold. The message continues.

"Mr. Oliver and I are leaving Mariposa on this morning's flight. We will not be returning."

"Ever," Kate says. She drops her head to the table.

I look over at Arya, she's staring at the phone and she looks like she's holding her breath.

"It didn't suit." Declan says over the voicemail, and in those three words I hear all the meaning buried within. I didn't suit. He's not *interested*. And somehow, he's convinced Percy that he isn't interested either.

"Discontinue the search for a property." Another pause. And even though I know he isn't going to say anything personal, and he certainly isn't going to say anything to me, this is a message on Kate's phone after all, I lean forward and wait for him to.

"That is all."

The message ends.

Kate bangs her head against the table another time. "My white whale," she moans. "I didn't even get the chance to catch him. I needed more time. I could've made him happy for a year. He was practically begging for a first wife."

I turn from Kate and look at Arya. She's staring out the kitchen window, looking confused and alone, just like she did at the beach on Rosa when Declan pulled Percy away.

There's a rush of anger, deep in my gut. Last night, when he refused to stop meddling in people's love lives, he practically told me this was going to happen.

He *told* me he was going to do this.

I reach over and put my hand on top of Arya's. She looks down when I squeeze her fingers, and she doesn't look back up.

After a few seconds of Kate thumping her head on the table and Arya's silence, Kate lifts her head and looks at me.

"La-La?"

"Yeah?"

She frowns at me. "What did you do to Declan last night?"

I raise my eyebrows.

What?

Kate sits up straighter and she narrows her red-rimmed eyes. I can see the wheels turning on her head.

"He was fine on the boat. Everything was going swimmingly. I was luring my whale in. Arya had a proposal all wrapped up. Then *you*"—she points at me —"toss him overboard—"

"I did not." I hold up my hands.

"And next morning, they've left the island. And will never return." She says "never return" with solemn finality. "So tell me. What did you do to Declan last night?"

Kate's lips are pursed and there's an unhappy wrinkle between her brows.

"Nothing," I say. "Absolutely nothing. Truly nothing."

Then I think of floating in the bioluminescence with Declan and our hands touching, and I think of him hammering my grandpa's shelf, and I think of him licking the apricot juice from his lips.

Nothing happened.

Then I hear Declan's voice in my mind saying, "Methinks thou protesteth too much."

I flush, suddenly hot and itchy.

Kate narrows her eyes.

"That's not nothing," she says, pointing at my cheeks.

I shake my head. "It's nothing. We argued. We always argue. I told him to stop meddling with true love. To leave Percy and Arya be. That's all."

Kate smacks her head. "You drove them away."

Arya interjects. "I think you're rushing to conclusions. Percy isn't like this. He wouldn't leave without letting me know. I'll call him."

Arya pulls her phone out and dials Percy's number. We wait until his voicemail picks up.

I can tell she's trying to sound upbeat and chipper. "Hi. It's me. I was just calling to let you know I'm excited to see you tonight. I can't wait." She stops for a second, then she says, "Okay. I...I'll see you tonight."

Arya hangs up.

"He'll call," I say, reassuring Arya.

Kate sighs, but at least she doesn't disagree.

"Of course he will," Arya says. She looks at her phone. "But just in the case, I'll text him too." She taps a message into her phone: see you tonight!

"He'll text," I say.

Arya smiles at me, confidence pasted over worry. "Of course he will."

Arya heads to work. Kate finishes off the fritters and then leaves at nine to drum up more clients to replace Declan and her missed opportunity, including the multi-million-dollar property sale.

I spend the day writing an article on local beach cleanup efforts. At eight o'clock, when the light's gone and the sun is down, Arya knocks on the door.

When I open it her mouth wobbles.

"He didn't call," she says.

I open the door wider.

"He didn't text," she says.

"He doesn't deserve you," I say.

She drops her head. "But he does. That's the horrible part. I threw out my list for him. I threw out my list."

I pull her in for a hug. I wrap her in my arms and hold her.

"I'm sorry, Arya. But honestly, he probably clips his toenails at the dinner table. You just didn't know him long enough to find out."

Arya pulls back and gives me a horrified look.

"Too soon?" I ask.

Then she lets out a half-laugh, half-sob. "No. Tell me more. Tell me all his fatal flaws."

I pull her inside and shut the door.

"I bet he never puts down the toilet seat, and he sprinkles wee on the rim, so that if you don't look when you sit, you fall into the toilet bowl like a slip 'n slide."

Arya considers this then nods. "Okay. What else?"

I think for a second.

"He has long black nose hair that he tweezes every morning and he leaves the hair all over the bathroom sink."

"Hmmm," Arya says. There's a bit of color re-entering her cheeks.

"How am I doing?" I ask.

"Not bad."

Good. I steer her toward the couch and then drop a chenille blanket onto her lap.

"He probably wears tighty whities," I say.

She takes this in, then shrugs. Apparently, tighty whities aren't a deal breaker for her. I sit down next to her on the couch and pull the blanket over my lap too.

"Anything else?" she asks. And I get the feeling that toenail clippings, lack of toilet etiquette, nose hair clippings and tighty whities aren't enough to ruin her image of Percy.

I drop my arm over her shoulder and give her a squeeze.

"Well, I didn't want to tell you this, but..." I pause.

"What?" she asks.

I smile and give her a confident, you're-better-off-without-him look.

"Well, the pièce de résistance," I say, "is that Percy has this creepy castle back in England, and he keeps his secret wife locked in the tower room, where she moans and lurks and freaks out visitors. It's weird and gothic. You really don't want to join her, locked up in the tower room."

"Your pièce de résistance is the plot from *Jane Eyre*?"

I shake my head. "No. It's the plot from Percy Oliver's life. It's his fatal flaw. Trust me. You do not want to go there."

Arya has the beginnings of a smile. "You're so weird."

"Do you feel better?" I ask hopefully.

She shakes her head. "Not at all."

I didn't think so.

So, we do the only thing that you can on the night when you're expecting a proposal and instead you get dumped. We call Kate and Renee and we make a boatload of margaritas.

15

I BEND OVER AND PICK UP ANOTHER PLASTIC BOTTLE FROM the rocky beach. My trash bag is nearly full. There are bottles, toothbrushes, shoes, plastic toys, and other random items that floated onto the little pebbled cove. I see that Arya, Kate and Renee have also nearly filled their trash bags.

It's nearing noon, the sky is cloudless, and the sun is high. It's about time we retreated to the shade. A trickle of sweat drips down my forehead and I swipe at it.

Michael is farther down the beach, standing on a sloping pile of coral rocks. When the waves roll over the rocks and then retreat, the rocks clank together and give off a tinkling, musical sound. He looks up, sees me watching, and waves at me. I wave back. I'm not sure this is exactly what he had in mind when he brought me the daisies, but he's been a good sport.

I promised everyone a picnic lunch at the cove if they

agreed to help with the cleanup. Trash floats in on the ocean currents and ends up on the shore of the island all the time. I like to do beach cleanups at least once a month, but I wanted to do another this weekend in penance for kicking off my shoes when Declan and I swam to shore.

Declan. Argh.

I've decided that the best way to deal with any thoughts of Declan Fox are to ignore them. Soon, I'll forget all about him. He came to the island, stayed for a short while, and then left.

In fact, he was sort of like a case of the chicken pox. He came, made me itchy and uncomfortable, and then he left. Now I'm immune to him. If he ever shows up again, I won't break out in itchy, unsightly bumps, I'll have no reaction to him at all. Pretty soon, I won't even think about him.

I wave at Michael again, probably more enthusiastically than necessary, and then bend down and grab a plastic container. I make sure to bend over as prettily as possible, making sure that Michael has a decent view.

"Did you crick your back?" asks Arya, coming up behind me. "Can't you stand up?"

I turn and squint up at her. The sun's getting really bright.

"Shhh," I say. "I'm trying to show off my bum for Michael." I wore cut-off jean shorts that show my curves when I bend over.

"Huh," she says. She looks at my butt and then turns back toward Michael. "He's not looking. He's talking to Kate."

"Oh." I humph and straighten up. Sure enough, Kate has her arm looped through his and she's leading him on a stroll across the coral rocks, pointing out sea fans and conch shells.

I stretch my back, arching backwards, and then roll my shoulders. Now that Arya mentions it, I am kind of sore from posing so long with my bum in the air.

"Can I ask you something," Arya says. She seems hesitant and a little embarrassed.

"Of course you can. You can ask me anything."

She fiddles with the drawstring of her bucket hat. Then finally she says, "Let's theoretically say that I sent Percy fifteen...no...seventeen texts and left three voicemails since he left..."

She tugs on her hat drawstring and looks dejected.

"Theoretically?" I ask.

She blows out a long breath then drops her hands to her sides.

"If I did happen to do that, and Percy didn't respond to any of them...what do you think is the probability that he either, a) died in a freak accident and would like to respond but can't because he's a ghost, b) was abducted by aliens and had a mind wipe so he can't remember me, c) received an urgent call to go on an Antarctic birding expedition and doesn't have reception to call me back, or d) he got all my messages, but won't respond because he actually didn't have any feelings for me, and I misread him, and he'd like me to stop texting and calling?"

I blink at Arya and try to assimilate everything she just said.

"Well? What do you think?" she asks.

I blink again and then say, "So...you're asking, what's the probability of a Percy ghost, an alien mindwipe, Antarctica or major jerkhood?"

"Yes," she says.

I think through the options and then say, "One percent, ten percent, point one percent and six percent."

Arya nibbles on her lip and tabulates my numbers. "Wait a minute. You think the alien mind wipe is most likely?"

I grin at her and look up at the sky. "Just think. Right now, Percy is having his brains shuffled around by little green men."

Arya punches my arm.

"Ouch." I rub my arm and stick my tongue out. "You asked."

She sighs. "I guess so. You think I should stop texting?"

I nod. "You should definitely stop texting."

"Stop texting who?" Renee comes up and drops her full trash bag onto the rocks next to us.

"Percy," I say.

Renee levels Arya with a firm, no-nonsense look. "Please tell me you haven't been blowing up his phone."

Arya looks down at her feet. "Only theoretically."

Renee snorts. Then she says, "Don't text him. Don't call him. Your dignity as a woman is on the line. Stop now."

Arya's shoulders slump. "But I love him," she whispers.

Ouch.

Renee shakes her head. "You loved that he loved

boobies. That's all Arya. That is all. Trust me, there are plenty of men in the world who love boobies."

Oh boy. "Not the time for booby jokes," I whisper.

But Arya snorts, then she starts to laugh. I look at her in surprise, because this is the first happy laugh she's given since Percy left.

Arya fell in love fast and hard. Hopefully she can fall fast and hard out of love.

"Can we have lunch now?" Renee asks. "I have about twelve hours of work to do today. I need some rum cake to fuel the hours of toil ahead."

"Definitely. But first"—I turn to Arya—"it's only been a short while. I don't think you were wrong about Percy. It was obvious to everyone that you two were meant for each other. Maybe he'll call. Maybe he'll be back. This could all be a misunderstanding."

She looks at me hopefully, "You think so?"

"No," Renee says. She tugs at the collar of her striped business shirt. Even on a beach cleanup day, Renee dresses like a lawyer. "He's ghosting you. He's either spineless or a prick."

Arya looks at me to see my response to Renee's assessment.

"I don't know," I say. "Sorry. I wish I had the answer."

"What would you do?" she asks.

I think about Declan, about how even though there was no love between us, and barely any like, I'm still feeling the hurt of his sudden departure. It was really unfair of him to come to the island, crash over me like a tidal wave and then retreat just as quickly without any preparation or goodbye.

"I'd forget about him," I admit. "As quickly as possible, I'd put him from my mind and move on with my life. Have beach cleanups and picnics."

"And cake and work," Renee says.

Then I add in my latest theory. "Just think of Percy like a case of the chicken pox. He made you feverish, itchy, blotchy and uncomfortable for a week, and then he disappeared. You may have a few pox scars, but you're immune to his brand of virus now and you can move on with your life and not fall for that type of love again. So. You're in the recovery stage. Just drink lots of fluids and take it easy."

"And don't call or text him. That's like trying to inoculate yourself again. It doesn't work," Renee adds.

I smile at her. "You like my metaphor?"

She quirks an eyebrow. "It works."

"What do you think?" I ask Arya.

She wrinkles her forehead and then says, "I think I want some cake."

Good enough.

We spread a blanket in the shade and I pull out a container of still warm jerk chicken, a tin of fried plantains, mango and chili salad, rum cake, and sweet tamarind and lime juice to drink. Kate and Michael wander over and Kate helps dish up the food and pass plates around.

Michael sits on the blanket next to me and leans back on his forearms. He tilts his head back and closes his eyes to enjoy the sun shining down on his face. The sea breeze ruffles his hair, and when he peeks his eyes open he catches me watching him.

I hold the plate in my hands out to him.

"Lunch," I say.

The skin around Michael's eyes crinkle when he smiles. "This looks delicious. You certainly know how to make a chap feel welcome."

"It's repayment for helping clean up the beach."

"Yet I was supposed to be apologizing for the boat incident," Michael murmurs. He tilts his chin down and looks at me ruefully.

"Maybe next time," I say with a smile.

His expression warms and he smiles back.

"This chicken is amazing," Renee says. She tears a chunk from the drumstick she's holding and pops it into her mouth.

"I just want cake," Arya says. She nibbles on a plantain.

"Are you planning on staying on the island long? Or are you leaving soon?" Kate asks.

Everyone stops eating and looks at Michael.

I wonder if he knows that Declan and Percy left. Probably. News travels fast on the island, even if you're only visiting.

Michael sits upright and looks at Kate with a friendly expression. "I find Mariposa to be full of wonderful scenery, wonderful company, and wonderful opportunities. I wouldn't dream of leaving soon."

He turns to me and winks.

I give him the "who me?" look and he grins in

response. If there's one thing you can say about Michael, it's that he doesn't beat around the bush.

After his announcement everyone goes back to eating. It's the best afternoon for a beach picnic, the sort of late February day that is temperate and beautiful and perfect for being on the shore.

Suddenly I feel like everything is going to work out.

Michael and I will continue to get to know one another. Percy will contact Arya and apologize for the misunderstanding. Kate will find a way to reunite with her family. Renee will get a promotion.

I lean over and whisper to Arya, "I just had a feeling that within a month, Percy will contact you."

She leans closer to me. "You think so?"

I give her a confident smile. "Definitely. How could he stay away?"

16

How could Percy stay away?

I'll tell you how.

With ease.

A week passes. Then two.

Soon a month has come and gone.

Percy doesn't call or text. And Arya doesn't get over him. As the days get brighter and hotter, she wilts, like a flower in the heat.

Watching her lose her vibrancy makes me feel helpless and angry. If I ever see Declan Fox again I'd love to shove him off one of his cargo boats into shark-infested waters and then give him a piece of my mind.

Luckily I was never in love or even in like with him. My chicken pox theory was right. I barely think of him except to hurl insults at him for hurting my friend.

Well, sometimes I think about him, but only when I

see an apricot, or a sailboat, or a coconut, or the stars, or...
anyway, I shove those thoughts away as quickly as possible.

Over the past month I managed to re-decorate the
guest bedroom with teal and coral highlights and rattan
furniture. Then I moved on to getting sweaty and dirty
planting a butterfly garden in the back.

Mostly, life is the same as it has always been.

Friends, work, renovations.

It's the same, but completely different.

Arya spends all her time at the nature preserve, and
when she's with us she's quiet and doesn't respond to any
of Renee's ribbing about boobies.

Kate claims she's forgotten about her plan to bag a
billionaire, but she's pre-occupied and often doesn't show
up to girls' nights.

Renee is busy with work. One of the seniors at her firm
had a paragliding accident, and she's taken on his
workload. She swears she'll be getting another promotion
any day.

Michael and I met for a few breakfasts and a lunch. A
few days ago he was called back to England, although he
promised to return as soon as possible.

I'm in my home office typing up an article on mangrove
preservation when my cell rings.

It's my mom.

"Isla, I'm glad you picked up." My mom has her
professor voice on, which means she means *business*.
Usually this has something to do with remembering to
have the cistern cleaned or checking the roof for hurricane
season.

"Hey Mom. What's up?" I smile and lean back in my desk chair.

"Do you remember my colleague, Doctor Racleaux from The University of Sheffield?"

I look up at the ceiling and shuffle through the dozens of researchers I've met over the years. I vaguely remember a short woman with orange hair who smelled of wet parchment paper.

"Yes? She studies Roman settlements in Britain?"

I think when I was nine or ten, we went on a tour with her of Vindolanda, an expansive Roman ruin in the English countryside.

"Precisely," my mom says happily. "I have wonderful news. She called last night. She remembered that you're a journalist with a more artistic bent than your father."

"That's a nice way of putting it," I say.

"She asked that you come out and visit for two weeks. Do in-person interviews, et cetera, she wants her biography done."

"Well..." My initial instinct is to say "thank you, but no thank you. I don't write biographies."

"All expenses paid, and a fair compensation."

"I don't think so. It's not really my cup of tea, and besides—"

"You'll stay at her country house near Vindolanda."

I stop talking.

So does my mom.

"That's too bad," she finally says. "Doctor Racleaux is such a nice woman. She remembered you fondly and wanted a writer she could trust—"

"Did you say Vindolanda?" I ask.

"Yes. It's in England, Isla. Don't you remember?"

I remember. I definitely remember.

I also remember that Vindolanda is near Newcastle.

Newcastle is where Michael is from. And Declan. And more importantly, Newcastle is less than an hour from Percy's country home. Where there are many, many birds. For all those avid bird watchers. Like Arya.

"Do you think Doctor Racleaux would mind if I brought a friend?"

"I don't see why not."

A happy smile spreads across my face.

Percy may not have come back to the island for Arya, but my hunch was right—within a month, everything would work out.

This is fate.

In less than a day it's all set. Arya and I are heading to England. We'll be staying for two weeks. I'll be researching and writing. Arya will be birdwatching. And if I have my way, she'll also "miraculously" run into Percy.

17

DOCTOR RACLEAUX—"CALL ME HARRIET"—IS EXACTLY AS I remembered. She's short, with orange hair that looks like fire coral, a large mole on her nose, and a green tweed skirt suit. She's nearing seventy, happily plump and reminds me of a teapot whistling out enthusiasm and good cheer.

"Are you dears settled?" she asks.

"We are. Thank you," I say. "This is really too much." I gesture at the lace-covered breakfast table.

It's the day after our transatlantic flight and Arya and I are having breakfast with Harriet in her solarium.

It's a huge spread, Harriet said it's a "full breakfast" as we need it to recover from jet lag.

There's a silver toast rack full of crusty toasted bread, fried eggs with crisp lacy edges, pork and sage sausages, thick pink back bacon dripping fat, broiled tomatoes, mushrooms, and saucy baked beans.

"Nonsense," Harriet says. "Your mother would have fits if she thought I wasn't caring for you properly."

To show that I'm in fact being cared for properly, I shovel as much breakfast onto my plate as possible. The sagey, peppery, savory smell rises up in the steam.

If I actually did have jet lag Harriet's cure would do the trick. I'll not share with her that as soon as I got on the plane I put on headphones, a mask, and knocked myself out into sweet, sweet oblivion. I slept from Mariposa straight through to London. I didn't wake up until Arya snapped my eye mask off my face and said, "Wake up sleepy head, we're here."

She didn't sleep at all. She was too worried about seeing Percy again, or even worse, not seeing Percy again.

Arya pokes at her fried egg with her fork and the bright sunshine yellow of the yolk pops and spreads over her plate.

The solarium is the brightest part of Harriet's old country manor. It has windows on three sides, looks out over her lush cottage-style garden, and is bright and airy. I'm sure on sunny days it's warm and bright. But this morning rain lashes against the glass and the sky is so gray that it's hard to tell how high the sun has risen.

"We only have two weeks for the interviews," Harriet says. She taps her spoon against the shell of a soft-boiled egg sitting in a porcelain egg cup. She smiles when the eggshell cracks and shows the milky white egg inside. "I'd prefer to begin immediately after breakfast, if that suits you. We can convene in the library."

I nod, unable to respond, because my mouth is full of

tomato and beans and toast. When I swallow I say, "That's perfect."

I'll bring my recorder and my laptop. And maybe a blanket or three, or four. It's a lot colder in England than I expected.

Granted, I looked at the weather and knew it would be rainy and chilly. It's March after all. But I didn't recall exactly what chilly felt like. It's a lot like *freezing*.

Yesterday, on the drive to Harriet's, Arya and I stopped at a little tourist shop (the only clothing shop we could find) and bought thick wool sweaters, wool pants, wool socks and wool scarfs. We're now both wrapped in more wool than three dozen sheep combined.

We showed up in long skirts and fuchsia and lime green colored tops with light raincoats. And now, we're wrapped in oversized dark green and brown sweaters, drab gray pants, thick socks, and scarves. We're like two parrots that traded in our feathers for the dull brown fluff of the wren.

"What are you going to do today, love?" Harriet asks Arya.

Arya sneaks a look at me. Even though I convinced her to come she's still not certain that approaching Percy is the best idea.

"I'd like to go birding," she says.

"What a delightful idea. Absolutely delightful. If you wait until the afternoon, I can take you to the Oliver estate on the coast. They have a spectacular nesting ground for seabirds."

"The Oliver estate?" I ask.

Harriet scrapes butter across a piece of toast and then piles on gooseberry jam.

"Oh yes. They open the coastal walk to the public one day a week. It's a pleasant spot for a picnic. No ruins there though." She says the last with a regretful frown, then she dismisses it and takes a happy bite of her gooseberry-slathered toast.

"We won't see the Olivers then?" Arya asks.

Harriet dabs her mouth with her napkin, catching a glop of gooseberry at the corner.

"No, no. The family resides in London."

"Oh. I see."

I'm not sure whether Arya is glad or disappointed by this news. But I'm not deflated. Fate wouldn't have put this trip into place if Arya wasn't meant to see Percy. He'll be there.

I eat the last of my breakfast, scraping my plate clean. The food is warm and filling. I think if I lived here, I'd eat this breakfast at least once a week. Probably twice.

Arya's poured herself a cup of coffee. Oh. Oh boy. I give a subtle shake of my head. She frowns. I gesture at my mug and make a no-no face. She shrugs.

Oh well.

It's not like I can tell her that Harriet's good English coffee tastes like muddy tap water run through an old man's boot.

"Do you have any tinned milk?" Arya asks.

"Tinned milk? Whatever for, dear?"

"My coffee?"

"Oh my, we have fresh cream or milk. Wouldn't you

prefer that? Do you only have tinned milk on the island? How sad."

Arya's eyes go wide. "Ummm. Hmmm."

She has no response. Apparently Harriet has never been introduced to the wonder of a spoonful of sweetened condensed milk in coffee.

Arya decides to drink the coffee black. I have the satisfaction of watching her mouth twist and her eyes nearly cross as she struggles with the decision of whether to spit it back into her mug or swallow.

She swallows.

I smile at her and tap the lip of my mug, then mouth, "Told you so."

Breakfast is finished. It's decided that Harriet and I will work until early afternoon, then we'll take a picnic to the Oliver estate.

I can barely believe it. We haven't been in England for forty-eight hours and everything is working out perfectly.

18

THE COAST IS BEAUTIFUL. IT'S SO VASTLY DIFFERENT FROM MY island home that I can barely take in the fact that I'm still on an island (albeit bigger) and still on a beach (albeit rockier).

Harriet pulls into the car park and turns off her little hatchback. The rain stopped earlier this morning, and while it's still wet and cold, it's no longer raining and wet and cold. In fact, the sun is almost peeking out from behind the now silvery clouds.

"Here we are," Harriet says happily.

I step out of the car onto the crushed gravel of the car park. The smell of sea air hits me. It's brinier than I'm used to, and also smells of wet rock and moss.

Arya tugs the large wicker picnic hamper out of the backseat. There's sausage rolls, coronation chicken, fairy cakes and cold drinks. Harriet said we need a full picnic lunch to keep up our energy for the long walk.

"This path leads to the nesting grounds." Harriet points to a small path meandering over lush green hills. She starts ahead of us at a brisk pace.

"Don't pet the sheep," she calls over her shoulder.

Arya snorts and hefts the basket in her arms. "We're wearing the sheep. Why would we pet them?"

I laugh.

"Come along," Harriet calls again.

Arya and I start down the path. It really is beautiful. The grass is fuzzy and emerald colored and sparkles from raindrops reflecting the slowly appearing sun. There are dozens of sheep milling around, white puffs dotting the landscape. And then there's the sea. It's dark gray, nearly black, and it rolls and rollicks right up to the shore.

"Are you nervous?" I ask.

Arya looks out over the water. "Very."

"You know, you don't have to try if you don't want to."

"I know. Don't worry about me. If nothing else, I'm going to see some amazing birds. See, it's a kittiwake." She points to a gull in the distance.

I don't think she wants to talk about how nervous she is, so instead, we talk about all the birds that she spots. When we finally catch up to Harriet, we try to find a somewhat dry patch of grass and set up our picnic lunch.

The sausage rolls are delicious, although I'm not too sure about the chicken. Arya quickly moves past the sausage and starts in on the fairy cake.

Harriet ignores the food and instead tells a story about finding a cache of Roman coins in a farmer's field.

"That should be chapter three," she tells me.

I get the feeling that Harriet doesn't care about the finished biography, she just wants to chat with someone about her life. She's nearing seventy and she's been married to her work her whole life. She has no husband, no children, no siblings, and her parents are gone. She's alone and she has no one to talk to.

The thought sends a queasy feeling through my stomach. That could be me someday. I could be the chatty older woman with no family, aching for someone to care.

"Isla." Arya pokes my thigh.

"Hmmm?"

"Isn't that Declan?" She points across the grass, down the shoreline.

I quickly turn to look. I've been complaining about the cold, but all of a sudden, I feel hot. As hot as if I were back in the bright sun on Mariposa. I can't see his face from this distance, but I know it's him.

His hands are in his pockets. He's wearing comfortable-looking jeans, leather boots, and an olive-green sweater. He walks with a casual stride and his head is turned toward the water. His black hair stands out against the silver gray of the sky. Somehow, he looks even better than he did on Mariposa, like he was born to tromp over open fields dotted with sheep, along rocky seaside beaches, and down worn walking paths lined with heather.

My heart thumps, and I set down the uneaten portion of my sausage roll. I don't think I'll be able to finish.

"Who's Declan?" Harriet asks. She perks up and looks across the field. "Do you know a gentleman in the area?"

"Declan Fox. He recently visited Mariposa." Arya says. Her voice is hopeful. Declan being here means that Percy is likely here too.

"Declan Fox, the shipping magnate?"

Arya nods. "That's right."

He's only about a hundred feet away. I can see his face more clearly. He looks different than he did on the island. More relaxed maybe. But lonelier too. Or maybe that's just me projecting.

He's walking closer. As he does, Arya says, "It's definitely him."

"Oh wonderful," Harriet says. Then she stands, waves her arms like a pheasant flapping in the brush, and calls in a high-pitched voice, "Hellooooo, Mr. Fox. Hellooooo."

He turns at her call and right away I see his shoulders stiffen. He pauses for a moment, stares at us, then turns to start walking again.

Arya snorts. "Definitely him."

I take in his stiff shoulders. "I don't think he recognizes us," I say quietly.

Arya and I both have rain hats on, even though it's not raining, long drab pants, and a double layer of wool sweaters. We're a thousand miles from where we were the last time he saw us. Literally and figuratively.

Harriet is not one to be dissuaded. "Mr. Fox, oh helloooo," she calls even more loudly. "Mr. Fox, your friends are here."

I look up at the wispy clouds in the sky and shake my head. When I look again, Declan's stopped and is sending a black look across the field at Harriet. His scowl is so ferocious that I can see it fifty feet away.

Apparently, though, Declan has better manners in England than he did in Mariposa, because he makes his way across the grass toward our picnic blanket. When he arrives at the edge of the plaid blanket he gives a short nod to Harriet and swiftly and disinterestedly runs his eyes over me and Arya.

"Ma'am. I'm sorry. I haven't had the honor," he says.

Sadly, even though his voice is stiff and brisk, it sends another rush of heat through me. And that's really, really unacceptable. I'd forgotten him. Hadn't I? I never liked him, right? So why, why am I getting all hot and bothered for him?

"Mr. Fox." Harriet straightens her back and pulls on the cuffs of her tweed coat. I think she's about to give him a lecture.

He raises his eyebrows. His eyes gloss over me again, probably only taking in the rubber hat and the shapeless sweater.

"I was just told the most fascinating thing. You recently stayed on Mariposa Island."

Declan looks back at the path, and I can tell he'd like to continue with his walk, away from the orange-haired, tweed-wearing, meddlesome woman.

"Yes," he says tersely. End of conversation.

Harriet smiles and then gestures at the picnic blanket. "I'm certain then, you'll want to join your friends from that same little island."

At her words Declan swings his gaze back to me. I tilt

my chin up and let him get a good look at me in all my damp, drab glory.

"Hello," I say.

I see the exact moment that Declan realizes it's me. If I wasn't watching closely I wouldn't have noticed any difference, but I am and I do. His eyes widen a fraction of an inch and darken from light green to a deep, dark, wild forest green, his lips fall open a tiny amount and he lets out a short, surprised puff of air. That's all. Those are the only indicators of any emotion at all. But on Declan they're the equivalent of someone else shouting, "What? Are you serious?! You're here?!"

He stares at me for a good five seconds. And I just lean back on the blanket and let him look his fill until the same old itch starts to travel over my skin. And now I realize what it feels like, it's not the itch of a new sunburn, it's the itch of a wool sweater rubbing over you. Declan itches like a wool sweater.

"You didn't say goodbye," I say.

Then I flush, because why did I say that?

Declan shakes his head, like a man shaking off after coming out of the water, and his eyes snap back to their normal shade.

"Apologies," he says.

"Join us," Harriet demands, and I realize that in thirty seconds flat she's decided that she's my matchmaker. "We're having a picnic and birdwatching."

She pats the blanket. Poor Harriet, she has no idea who she's up against.

"I apologize. I haven't the time—"

"Sit down," she interrupts in a firm headmistress voice I recognize from my mom. Apparently all professors, researchers and teachers can emulate that "obey me, or else" tone.

Declan sits down. In fact, he sits down on the blanket so quickly that I nearly do a double-take.

I take it back. Harriet doesn't need to know who she's up against. She's a bulldozer.

Arya gives Harriet an appalled look. She's set down the fairy cake she was gobbling and looks a little pale. Maybe the stress of an imminent meeting with Percy is giving her intestinal distress.

Harriet beams at Declan and pulls out a paper plate from the picnic hamper. She stacks a sausage roll, coronation chicken and a pile of chips onto it, then she hands it to Declan.

"Eat," she says.

And he does. Although while he's taking a bite of the chicken he looks at me as if he doesn't quite understand how he came to be sitting on a plaid picnic blanket, eating mayonnaise-slathered chicken.

"I'm Doctor Harriet Racleaux, famed researcher, I'm sure you've heard of me..." Harriet pats her orange hair and looks at Declan expectantly.

"No, I—"

"But enough about me. My dear Isla is writing an entire biography detailing my accomplishments. You can read it when it comes out. Tell me about you. How did you find Mariposa? Is it as charming and delightful as Isla leads me to believe?"

Declan has a mouthful of coronation chicken. He stops chewing at that and stares in consternation at Harriet.

I wonder if he has the gall to tell her that he didn't find anything of "interest" there.

She claps her hands and Arya jumps in surprise.

"Mr. Fox is speechless. I knew it was beautiful. I knew it."

"Mmm," Declan says through his mouthful of mayo.

I hold back a snort but can't manage to cover the little noise of disbelief that comes out.

Declan looks at me and raises an eyebrow. I'm sure it's meant as a silent reproach, but the brisk sea breeze ruffles his short hair and his cheeks are pink from his walk, and I decide he looks too boyish for any reprimanding.

"Isn't that wonderful," Harriet continues. She takes the spoon from the bowl of chicken and drops another large scoop of curry mayo-coated chicken onto Declan's plate. "I've always wanted to visit, but as you know, I'm a world-renowned researcher and there are no Roman ruins on Mariposa. My fame directs my schedule, alas." There's a distinct twinkle in Harriet's eyes when she says this, and I get the feeling she's having a good laugh on the inside.

I put my hand over my mouth to hide my smile.

Harriet keeps on talking about Mariposa and how much Declan must've loved it. There hasn't been space for him to respond, not that he's wanted to. Instead, he's been watching me.

"Tell me, what did you like most?" Harriet asks.

Declan's mouth is full of chicken, but instead of

swallowing and answering, he grabs a chip and shoves it in his mouth. He crunches noisily.

I raise my eyebrows at him. Unbelievable.

He watches me the entire time he chews. I try not to squirm. Honestly, his gaze is disconcerting.

So, I turn away from him and address Harriet. "I don't think Declan cared for Mariposa." I give her an apologetic shrug. "The hot sun, clear seas, and slow, tropical days were not to his taste."

Harriet wrinkles her forehead and the wind blows briskly so that it looks like her hair is standing up in surprise. "Truly, that doesn't..." begins Harriet.

Declan clears his throat. "On the contrary, I found it very much to my taste."

He...what?

I turn back to him, but I can't read his expression.

"Really?" I ask skeptically, remembering his voicemail for Kate and of course, all the conversations he and I had. "I find it surprising that your opinion concerning the ordinary pleasures made such an about turn."

"I've felt this way for some time now," he says.

Harriet looks between the two of us like she's watching a tennis match.

I feel myself starting to flush, so I scowl at him.

"Is Percy here?" Arya asks abruptly. She wipes the fairy cake crumbs off her wool pants.

Declan turns to Arya and I don't see anything in his expression that speaks to guilt or remorse.

"No. He's not."

Declan says this with cold finality so it's no surprise that Arya flinches. The way he said "he's not" implied that she shouldn't get her hopes up. Ever.

"Shame. The young ladies will be here for two weeks." Harriet dangles that tidbit out for Declan to grab ahold of.

He doesn't.

Instead, he sets his plate down on the blanket and says, "Thank you for the delicious meal and the pleasant company."

"Surely, you don't have to leave so soon?" Harriet says.

"I do. It was a pleasure." Declan takes Harriet's hand and gives her a polite parting shake. Then he says, "Arya. Isla."

And that's that. He's already walking away.

I didn't even have the chance to say goodbye.

Harriet sighs. "What a specimen. I'll bet my eyeteeth that he has the blood of the Roman invaders. Well, plenty of us do, but still."

Harriet follows Declan's retreating form. She seems smitten. Arya, unfortunately, looks almost as bad as she did the day Percy left. I think she must've been holding tightly onto the hope that we'd see Percy, and now Declan's shattered it.

Which reminds me...

"I'll be right back," I say, then I run after Declan.

I race down the path. My boots thump over the dirt and grass as I chase him down.

"Hey, wait up."

The breeze is stiffer along the path, since it's closer to

the shore, and it carries my voice away. Declan doesn't notice me until I'm next to him.

I tug on his sleeve, and when he sees it's me the side of his mouth turns up. "Yes?"

I ignore the flushing of my cheeks and poke at his arm. "Are there any sharks here?"

Clearly that's not what he was expecting me to say.

He shakes his head. "What?"

I point at the gray, surf painted water. "Sharks. Here."

He narrows his eyes on me. "Why?"

"Because I'd love to feed you to them."

A slow grin spreads over his face. And I have the realization that he really is one of the most magnetically attractive people I've ever met. His smile hits me low in my belly, so I clench my fists and fight the urge to lean toward him.

"Are you truly so upset that I didn't say goodbye?" he asks. There's a gleam of amusement in his eyes.

"Ha. I couldn't care less. You not saying goodbye has nothing to do with feeding you to ravenous sharks."

His smile grows broader. I've never seen him smile so much, and it's doing funny things to my insides. "Stop smiling at me," I say.

His eyes crinkle. "That's my line."

He starts to walk down the path again and I hurry to keep up. "Hey. Stop. You did it again. You can't just leave in the middle of a conversation, or the middle of an acquaintance. You have to say something like "goodbye," or "nice knowing you," or "talk to you soon." Stop walking so fast."

I'm nearly jogging to keep up with him.

"I have a meeting," he says. "I merely came out to clear my head."

He looks down at his watch. I barely notice the watch, what I do notice is the solidness of his wrist, the muscles of his forearm, the dusting of dark hair...I yank my gaze up.

"Are you staying at Percy's place?" I ask abruptly.

It's likely since there aren't any other homes within walking distance. The Oliver ancestral home is a fourteenth century stone manor house that sits high up on a hill overlooking the sea. Harriet told us all about it on the drive over.

"I am," he says.

"That's another thing—" I begin but Declan cuts me off.

"Isla, I have to go. How about we say goodbye now?"

We're at the base of the hill where the private gated path turns up to the manor.

No, a voice inside me says. I don't want to say goodbye.

"I'm not done yet," I say.

Declan reaches forward and tugs on the bulky fabric of my layered wool sweaters. His eyes light with amusement. "Are you cold?"

I scowl at the heat of his fingers against my wrist and the buzz going through me.

"No," I say. It's the truth, I haven't been cold since I saw him walking down the path.

His pointer finger touches the center of my wrist, right above my pulse point. He leaves it there for a moment and my subconscious decides I've given it permission to pick up its fantasies where they left off a month ago.

But instead of sandflies on the beach, I'm imagining rolling around on the grassy, heather-scented hillside, sheep baaing noisily while Declan drags his hands over my bare skin. I'm not cold in my imagination either.

"Why are you here?" he asks, dragging me out of the (unwelcome) fantasy.

My mind's as fuzzy as the wool sweater I'm wearing. I try to form a coherent answer.

"Well, Mr. Fox, it's either to stalk you or research a book assignment. Take your pick."

"Hmm." He gives me a slow look and his eyes turn lush forest green again. "Goodbye, Isla."

Argh. His goodbye hits me in the gut. How unfair.

"You deserve to be tossed to the sharks," I say. "Arya's heart is broken. I won't stand aside and let you—"

"Can I see you again before you leave?" he asks.

Wait.

"You...what?"

He steps back and clasps his hands behind him. "You have more to say. I could come by and see you."

This is so strange. I'm in a world where Declan Fox is voluntarily coming to see me.

But slowly I nod. "That's a good idea."

He opens the gate then says, "I thought so."

It clatters shut behind him. He doesn't turn around as he strides up the path.

"Now is when you say goodbye," I shout after him.

"Like, see you later. Au revoir. Ciao. Hasta luego. Goodbye!"

He doesn't respond, but I think I see his shoulders shaking with laughter. I refuse to acknowledge that his amusement makes me happy. When he comes by I'm going to convince him to help reunite Percy and Arya.

That's all.

19

AFTER A FULL WEEK IN ENGLAND, I'VE SPENT NEARLY ONE hundred hours interviewing Harriet and recording her life story. We haven't had any more birding outings or picnics, we've just been cloistered in her bookshelf-lined library taking a fine-toothed comb to her memories, her journals, her photographs and her articles. We've finally made it to the two thousands. The beginning of her "prolific" phase.

I'm in the overstuffed chintz chair near the fireplace, a wool blanket in my lap, tapping in notes on Harriet's story. The library is about the size of my living room, but it doesn't have any windows, just walls lined with shelves chock-full of books, journals, artifacts, and random pieces of paper stuck in between the pages of books and under Roman helmets or pottery. Harriet sits on the plaid loveseat across from me, although whenever she gets to an exciting part in her stories, she hops up and paces back and forth across the thinning carpet. The library is a well-loved, well-used room.

"Now, the farmer was named Reginald Hog, the perfect moniker for a pig farmer if you ask me, and he raised Gloucester Old Spots. That was the type of pork in the sausages we had yesterday, dear."

I nod and try to keep my eyes from crossing. We've been working since seven this morning and it's nearing three in the afternoon. We had a working lunch, and I don't expect we'll be stopping until eight for a late dinner.

I think Harriet keeps herself going with pots and pots of black tea and plates of crumbly shortbread.

"One day, when his prize boar was hoofing about in the pen, it pulled up a lump of something unusual."

"An artifact?" I ask. If I remember correctly, the Hog field discovery was Harriet's greatest find.

She jumps up from the couch. "That's right. A small piece of pottery. No bigger than your thumb."

She hurries over to her walnut secretary desk and begins riffling around. "I know it's here somewhere. Just a moment."

I stare at the empty fireplace. Arya's out at the coast again. She's spent the entire week wandering the Oliver estate cataloguing birds. Unfortunately, I've come to the conclusion that it wasn't fate that pulled us here, it was coincidence. And now, my wrongheaded certainty has turned Arya into some tragic, gothic heroine that paces the moors in a flowing white dress, pining for her lost love. Except, she's wearing bulky drab sweaters instead of a dress. And it's modern day. But still. The metaphor works.

I'm an idiot for bringing her here.

I'd hoped that Declan would come by. I could badger him into helping reconnect Arya with Percy.

That hope was dashed when I realized he wasn't actually going to show.

"And that's how I uncovered a treasure trove of Roman pottery in a farmer's field. Fascinating, isn't it?" Harriet stops in front of me with a beatific smile.

I blink at her, then reach down and press stop on my recording. "You are incredible," I say. And I mean it, even if I didn't hear the last bit of her story. "I just need a moment to go to the bathroom."

I can take a minute, rewind the recording and catch up.

"Wonderful idea. I'll put on the kettle for a spot of tea."

Hmm. On Mariposa, when a tropical storm or hurricane is on the way, all the Brits run to the store and stock up on boxes and boxes of tea and loads of chocolate biscuits. I always wondered why. Who could possibly drink hundreds of bags of tea during a storm? Now I know. Harriet could.

There's a soft chiming sound, a ding dong ding. I look around the library.

"That's the front door," Harriet says. "I'll just go see who's popped round."

I hurry to the bathroom, put in my earbuds, and push play on the recorder. Three minutes later I'm all caught up. I splash my face with ice-cold water, pinch my cheeks and hop a bit on my toes so that I can stay awake the rest of the afternoon.

When I come out, Harriet's waiting in the hallway. She

has flushed cheeks, and her hair stands up on end. She's so excited that she reminds me again of the boiling teapot about to whistle from all the bubbling steam.

"Everything alright?" I ask.

She puffs out her cheeks and flaps her hands in front of her. "Your Mr. Fox has come calling."

Oh. Not what I was expecting. My mind goes blank at the same time as my body goes all liquidy and warm. My subconscious pulls out images of apricots. Weren't there apricots in the coronation chicken too? Does he like apricots?

Argh. It doesn't matter what he likes.

"He's not my Mr. Fox," I say.

Then I feel ornery because Harriet's excitement dims. But then she rallies. "I've put him in the solarium with a pot of tea and fresh scones, with jam and clotted cream."

I give her a small smile. "That's really nice."

She pats my arm. "I'll let you have a nice chat. I'm sure you need a break. I've been rambling for hours—"

"You don't ramble."

"And hours. I do. It's fine. Needs must make time for love though."

She winks at me, and I get the feeling that she's imagining Declan and I had a torrid affair in Mariposa and now that we've unexpectedly reunited we're about to get all hot and heavy in her solarium.

I stare after her then let out a long sigh.

Well, he came.

I run my hands through my hair, then self-consciously pull it over my shoulder. I'm in a brown wool sweater, baggy gray slacks and nubby socks. Oh well, it is what it is. It's not as if we're actually about to get it on in the solarium. The only thing I want to do is talk to Declan about Percy and Arya.

With that in mind I square my shoulders, put my chin up and march into the solarium.

Declan sits on the couch near the window. There's a pot of tea, two tea cups and a plate of scones on the coffee table in front of him.

I clear my throat and he quickly looks up. When he sees me he stands.

I stop walking, suddenly incredibly uncomfortable.

"Hello," he says. His voice is low and intimate.

My word. My word.

Why does he have to look so beautiful? He's in a navy pinstripe suit with a crisp white shirt. It's perfectly tailored. He's shaved, his hair's been trimmed since last week. He looks...argh, he looks like a classy businessman bazillionaire. How am I supposed to badger him and yell at him now?

"Is everything all right?" he asks.

I'm still standing in the entry, completely without words.

"Fine. Amazing," I say. Then I frown down at my mud-brown sweater.

He gestures to the coffee table set up with scones and tea.

"Harriet was kind enough to..." He stops talking when I walk around the dining table and join him at the little couch by the window.

"Please," he says, gesturing to the couch.

He waits until I sit before he joins me.

Okay. So, my plan was to march in here and blame him for my friend becoming a gothic zombie pacing the metaphorical moors. But now...I can't.

My body vibrates with this warm tension, and the air feels thick and slow. It's hard to pull in a full breath. The couch is old and the cushions bow to the middle. I unintentionally slide closer to Declan and my thigh rubs against his.

He stiffens, almost imperceptibly.

He clears his throat again and looks at me from the side of his eyes. He feels it too. I know he does.

That doesn't make it any better though.

We both stare at the tea and scones, not saying anything. Unfortunately, it's one of those situations where the longer silence goes on, the more awkward it becomes.

Yet, I can't bring myself to say, "Why the heck did you drag Percy away, you Neanderthal?"

"Tea?" he asks, breaking the silence.

I'd like to say, "I don't want tea, I want you to stop being a meddling prick."

Instead, I nod then lick my dry lips. "Please."

He reaches forward and I watch as he lifts the flower-stenciled teapot to pour us both a cup of tea. I never noticed how long his fingers were, or how the tendons on the back of his hands belie his strength.

When he's finished I reach forward and take a sip of the steaming liquid. It's Darjeeling, Harriet's favorite.

"Thank you," I say, after I've had a taste.

He nods and we both sit in silence while we sip the tea. A minute passes, then two. I can't take it anymore. The tension, the warm, magnetic pull vibrating between us.

I have to say something. "It was horrible what you did—"

"I have to tell you, when I said I believed in love at first sight—"

We both start and then stop at the same time.

I blink, unsure what he's going to say. Something about love.

"Please. Go ahead," he says.

I shake my head, embarrassed to have started in on him without warning. "No, I'm sorry. What were you saying?"

I turn my knees toward him and they brush against him. He looks down at where we're touching and then back at me.

"You remember when I said I believed in love at first sight?" he asks.

I nod. There's a weird electric tingle traveling over me. "With Vicky."

Declan lifts the edge of his lip. "Not Vicky."

Huh. "Okay?"

He looks at me like I'm missing the point.

"You," he says.

"Me?" What in the heck is he talking about? He believes in love at first sight with...the tingle turns to a jolt and I sit up straight.

"Me?" I say more forcefully.

"You."

That warm tingle is doused by the bucket of ice water that is the word *you.*

Declan Fox loves me?

Me?

He stands and paces to the other side of the room. He runs a hand through his short black hair, messing up the neat trim, making him look more human. He turns around and he looks almost as if he's in pain, and then I notice that he has bags under his eyes and he looks tired and conflicted.

"You love me," I say. Just to confirm. The words taste weird in my mouth.

Declan rubs his hand down his face then nods. "I know. It doesn't make sense."

I frown at him. "You think?" I say, and I don't think he hears the warning in my voice. I remember the first time he saw me. It was at the Valentine's Day brunch when he mocked me and called me a pathetic, sad, single woman. Love at first sight my foot.

"You're not as attractive as the women I typically date," he says.

He gestures at me, like me and my ugly brown sweater are exhibit A. My eyes widen at the train wreck of Declan's declaration.

He starts pacing again.

"You aren't as ambitious or as well-connected."

Excuse me?

"Right."

He doesn't seem to realize that I spoke through gritted

teeth. In fact, he seems to think that we're on the same wavelength.

He gives me a pained, beseeching look. "I date CEOs, the daughters of dukes, politically and socially connected women."

Are you kidding me?

"I see." My hands curl into the wooly fabric of my sweater and I clench the material tightly.

He stops his pacing and faces me full on. "It doesn't make sense. You don't bring anything to the table. In fact, it would be lunacy to marry you."

Whaaaa? I drop my hands from my sweater. The word *marry* tumbles around in my head until it comes to a crashing stop.

Declan wants to... "Marry?" I choke out.

He gives a sharp nod. I suddenly have the overwhelming urge to drag him outside and find a shark pool to toss him into.

"The second I saw you, wobbling through the sand, your laugh as bright as the sun, your face covered in chocolate, I knew. You were the one. I said to myself, Declan, if you don't marry that girl, you're an idiot."

Oh my gosh.

He and I definitely have a different memory of that day. Vastly different.

"Then I heard your friends talking at your table. Wanting to bag me." He gives me a black look, like Kate and her white whale obsession was all my fault. "Needless to say, I reacted badly."

He reacted...badly.

Wait a minute. "You didn't hear them until the airport," I say. Even though I was all woozy that day, I clearly remember our conversation on the plane.

"I heard them for the second time at the airport," he says.

Which means, from the moment he met me, he knew we "planned" to lure him in and "bag him."

"Fine," I say.

We stare at each other, Declan with a conflicted, hungry look on his face. And me, I imagine I just look cranky.

Marry.

My subconscious latches on to the sparkly word and adds a wedding dress to my apricots on the beach and sheep in the heather fantasies. I slam the door on that thought. Just because I find him inexplicably attractive doesn't mean he's marriage material.

Declan agitatedly runs his hand through his hair again, messing it up even more. It reminds me of how he looked when I woke up on top of him. Sleep-mussed and attractive. Until he ruined it by telling me to get off of him.

He looks at me and his eyes are beseeching. "You aren't who I would've chosen for myself, but I can't get you out of my mind. Your laugh, your humor, your perspective on life —everywhere I turn, you're there. You consume me. I persuaded Percy not to make such a monumental mistake as marry a woman out for his status, but I can't do myself the same favor."

He's admitted it. He purposely ruined Percy and Arya's relationship. And now he wants to...marry me?

Because I consume him?

An apparently pseudo-attractive, unconnected, unappealing, status-seeking woman?

Plus, he still thinks I want him for his status?

No. Oh no. Nuh uh. No.

I see red.

I always thought seeing red was a made-up thing. I never believed people actually saw red when they were angry. Well they do. For a split second my whole vision turns bright angry red.

When my vision clears Declan is standing in front of me.

"Would you..."

"No."

He stops. "You haven't let me ask the question."

I shake my head. "No. Whatever it is, no."

"Isla," he says, and the way he says it has me grinding my teeth.

"No."

He considers this and then says, "What if I wanted to give you my fortune?"

"No."

"An island?"

"No."

"A home on the beach?"

"No."

"A yacht?"

I dig my nails into my palms. "No. Not even if you offered me the moon."

He looks lost for a moment and I almost feel sorry for him. Except, I don't.

I stand and tilt my chin to meet his gaze.

"You're unbelievable," I say.

He's stunned. Good.

I poke him in the chest, right against his crisp white shirt.

"What's wrong with you? I won't date you. I won't marry you. I won't...anything with you. You're horrible."

Declan's lips turn down into a sharp frown. I don't care.

"You treated me horribly on Mariposa, insulting me at every turn. Then, you left without saying goodbye, dragging Percy away, wrecking my friend's hopes and breaking her heart. Arya's a good person. Decent and kind and she loves Percy. He won't find a more honest, better person than her. Well done. You ruined a good thing because of your conceit and pride and inability to see other's as they really are."

Declan leans forward, his jaw tight and his eyes stormy. "Is that all?"

I refuse to step back. "No. Definitely not." I gesture around the room. "You come here, apparently to profess your love but instead of telling me why you love me you tell me why you shouldn't love me and all the things that are wrong with me. Why would that entice me to marry you? It wouldn't. A billion dollars can't compensate for being a jerk."

He swallows and takes a step back. "I see. You don't reciprocate my feelings."

My stomach goes queasy. I don't like seeing his face

close off and return to the look he wore when we first met. But what can I do? He's not a good person.

"No," I say, and my stomach drops like a diving airplane. "If your horrible recitation of why I'm not good enough for you wasn't enough to turn me off, then your initial treatment of me was. Beyond that, you ruined my friend's happiness. And equally bad, you stole Mr. Sherman's pension, he was an old man for crying out loud. And then you attempted to ruin Michael's life, and you nearly did when you caused the end of his engagement with his fiancée. I can't say that there's anything about you that would recommend me to marry you, date you, or even like you. So please, stop thinking of me, stop being consumed by me, just stop, it's not reciprocated. Not at all."

There.

It's said and done.

I cross my arms and try to ignore the churning in my stomach and the sharp aching in my chest.

Declan doesn't speak. He merely stares at me for a good fifteen seconds, completely silent. His irises have shifted to icy cold, like freezing rain sleeting over green hills.

I get the feeling that I won't ever be seeing him again. Not after what I've said.

I almost want to take my words back. Almost. But what I said about him being awful is the truth, and you can't hide away the truth.

Finally, Declan nods, and I feel that he's filed me away in a closed off part of his mind. The part he doesn't visit. Ever.

"That's how you feel," he says.

It's not a question. Still, I say, "It is."

"You don't care for me."

I swallow. There's a lump the size of an apricot in my throat. "Not really."

He tilts his head and little brackets form around the tense edges of his mouth. "I suppose this is where we say goodbye then."

He holds out his hand.

I look at it for a moment, hanging between us. Take it, Isla, I chide myself, take it. He's finally saying a proper goodbye.

I reach out and slip my hand into his.

My chest pinches at the contact. He's warmer than I remember. Except, he was warm that night on the island, wasn't he?

Oh gosh. Maybe I like him a little. He has some good qualities.

No, Isla, stay strong. He's a beast.

"Goodbye," he says.

"Goodbye."

He drops my hand.

I don't say anything more as he walks out of my life.

20

If Harriet was hoping for a tale of declarations of love and romance, she was sorely disappointed. We worked nonstop for the next six hours. When Arya came back from her birding, she was so rumpled and downtrodden looking that I decided not to bother her with the details of Declan's visit.

We had a late dinner of steak and kidney pie, which I will never, ever eat again, and then called it a night.

Now, it's two in the morning, and I still, still can't sleep. I might blame it on the brightness of the full moon shining through the window, or the hissing and popping of the radiator, or the squeaking of the old mattress every time I flip over. I could easily blame it on any of those things. But the truth is, I can't sleep because I can't stop rewinding through all the times I was with Declan, and rewriting the script with the new knowledge that he loved me.

Loved me.

Unwilling or not, he loved me.

That pompous, arrogantly rude man at the Valentine's Day brunch? It was a man who fell in love at first sight and then heard he'd fallen for a "gold digger."

The conversation on the plane, my attempt to get him to kayak with me to the island. All of it is colored differently when I look at it from his perspective.

I remember what I said that day on the beach before we kayaked out to the little island. "You've already fallen for me. It's just sad, because you don't know it yet. Your itty bitty wittle brain is having trouble assimilating what your stone-cold heart already knows. That you looove me."

He scoffed and said, "That'll be the day." But he was hiding the truth that he knew he loved me, that apparently he'd fallen for me from the first.

And I replied, "Don't worry Declan, someday you'll beg me to marry you. It'll be grand."

Well, he did. And it wasn't grand. Not at all.

I think about how he held me on the island during the storm, let me sleep on him, how he jealously asked me to dance at the gala, how he jumped in after me when I fell off the sailboat, how he floated with me in the bioluminescence pool, and then fixed my grandpa's bookshelf.

All of it is colored differently and reframed.

I tug at the quilted duvet and pull it over my chin. The window of the little dormer guest room I'm in constantly leaks in the chill spring air. The mattress springs squeak as I pull the duvet higher.

Declan loved me.

And I suppose, he hated that he fell in love at first sight, because I was a possible gold digger, and I wasn't at all like the women he usually dated. His mind chose one type of woman, but his heart chose another. I can see that being difficult for someone like him.

I frown at the milky light filtering past the toile curtains. I can see the moon hovering over the trees of the nearby woods.

"Maybe he has a point," I say.

The moon doesn't have an answer. So I reply for it, "No. He doesn't."

Perhaps he did keep me warm on the island, and try to rescue me after I fell off the sailboat, and he did fix my grandpa's shelf and he was sweet when I made him dinner...but, and this is a big but, he ruined Mr. Sherman's life, he ruined Michael's relationship, and he ruined Arya and Percy's chances.

So it doesn't matter how the past is reframed. It doesn't matter that my skin goes itchy and uncomfortable when he's around and my subconscious dreams up fantasies. It doesn't matter if he loved me at first sight. He can fall out of love.

I sigh and punch my pillow, trying for the nine thousandth time to get comfortable. It's quiet in the wrong way here. I need the island's evening chorus of whistling frogs, like crickets but sweeter, droning on through the night. The "Declan movie" as I've dubbed it starts to play again. The tape of our first meeting begins.

I fling the duvet back. "No thank you."

I step onto the chilly wood floor and scrunch my toes

back. There's no helping it. I get out of bed and walk over to the little secretary desk where my laptop is. It's nearly three now, I'm not any closer to sleep, so I may as well work. I have hours and hours of Harriet's interview notes to organize.

Roman artifacts are certain to distract me. The blue light of my laptop screen glows as I open my email. Harriet promised to scan and send me some documents.

I pause.

There at the top of my inbox is an email from Declan.

He sent it only ten minutes ago.

He can't sleep either?

My skin tingles and I look around the room. Why do I feel like he's here watching me? I take a deep breath and slowly blow it out. It doesn't make me feel any better.

My hand hovers above the keyboard. There isn't a subject line to the email and for some reason I'm scared to open it. What could he have to say? Wasn't this afternoon goodbye?

But I'm not a coward. So I hold my breath and open his letter.

It's long.

That's the first thing I notice.

Then I read the first sentence.

ISLA,

I'm not writing to reiterate what I said today, or ask you to reconsider, there's no need to be concerned.

. . .

I LET OUT MY BREATH. "I'M NOT CONCERNED," I SAY. I KEEP reading.

I ALSO WON'T DEFEND MY ACTIONS SEPARATING PERCY FROM Arya. I acted with the best intentions, and with the knowledge that I have I wouldn't act differently, even now. I wouldn't be a true friend if I let Percy pursue a woman who spoke of "bagging the white whale" without voicing my opposition.

"THAT'S BECAUSE YOU'RE HORRIBLE," I SAY. "ODIOUS, AND arrogant and prideful and..." I scroll down and keep reading.

BUT IN REGARD TO MR. SHERMAN AND MICHAEL, I CANNOT, will not, continue to accept your blame and derision.

"WHY NOT? YOU ADMITTED TO HAVING DONE IT," I SAY. IT'S like he hears me, because he writes:

I DID ADMIT THAT I WAS SORRY FOR HAVING ENTERED INTO A partnership with Mr. Sherman. But not because of any wrong on my part, only for the lesson I learned. That those we trust as friends are not always friends, and they don't always have the best intentions.

. . .

I FROWN AT HIS WORDS. I'M NOT SURE WHAT HE MEANS.

*S*HORTLY *INTO OUR VENTURE, I LEARNED M*R. *S*HERMAN *WAS funneling all the business profits into high-risk ventures, gambling, and other habits. The profits I believed we had were in fact debts. Needless to say, I discontinued our partnership, paying Mr. Sherman his initial investment back. Then I worked tirelessly to come back up from the deep hole my misplaced trust put me in. I never shared the circumstances of our dissolved partnership, out of respect for an old family friend.*

I STARE AT DECLAN'S WORDS, TRYING TO ASSIMILATE WHAT he's saying.

"You're not a pension thief," I say. My cheeks go hot when I realize how many times I judgmentally accused him of being one. Did Michael not know? I lean forward in my desk chair and scroll down the email.

*I*N *REGARD TO M*ICHAEL'S *FIANCÉE.*

"RIGHT. EXPLAIN THAT," I SAY, AS IF DECLAN'S HERE IN front of me. Michael's situation is just like Arya's. Declan ruined true love because of his weird fixation on thwarting gold diggers.

. . .

MICHAEL NEVER HAD A FIANCÉE.

"WHAT?" I QUICKLY COVER MY MOUTH, BECAUSE IT CAME out as a loud, surprised squeak.

VICKY WAS MY FIANCÉE.

OH MY GOSH. HOLY UNBELIEVABLE. VICKY. THE VICKY. THE Vicky that Percy was cajoling Declan to get over.

AFTER MR. SHERMAN'S FUNERAL, MICHAEL ATTEMPTED TO exhort more funds from my business. His reasoning was that I wouldn't be where I was without his father. When I disagreed, Michael decided to find funds another way, by seducing my fiancée. He is known to seduce well-connected, wealthy women for money and advancement. I paid him the amount he asked in exchange for leaving my fiancée alone and out of the tabloids. I hadn't seen him again, not until the night of the gala.

"THAT'S...THAT'S..." THE DETAILS OF THAT NIGHT RUN PAST me. Declan's cold anger. Michael's charming smile. His smirk when I denied Declan a dance and he led me away. Then I remember Declan telling me to be careful on the sailboat. Maybe he wasn't talking about the edge of the platform. Maybe he was talking about Michael.

. . .

I DIDN'T WRITE THIS LETTER TO CHANGE YOUR MIND OR YOUR feelings toward me. I understand that door is closed. I merely wanted to correct a misunderstanding. I hold you in high regard, and I admit, it hurt my pride that you think so little of me.

FOR SOME REASON MY HEARTBEAT THUMPS LOUDLY IN MY ears and I suddenly feel ill. Like that steak and kidney pie has gone bad in my stomach.

I WISH YOU THE BEST IN YOUR ENDEAVORS. PLEASE DON'T BE concerned, I won't bother you again.

I SIT FOR FIVE MINUTES, TEN, JUST STARING AT THE computer screen. I can't believe it. He wasn't...he wasn't ever the arrogant, prideful, pension-stealing, love-ruining villain I painted him to be.

I told him that he ruined relationships by refusing to see people as they really were. But isn't that what I did to Declan? And Michael too? I painted Michael as a charming, saintly, potential love interest. I misjudged him as well.

My nausea has passed. Now I just feel numb.

I was prejudiced against Declan from the very start and I never gave him a fair chance. Even when he was telling me that he loved me, I saw his declaration through a lens of prejudice. I know he's right. I'm certain I'm not as connected as the women he typically dates, nor am I a model, nor the CEO of a company, nor the daughter of an aristocrat. He could easily have any of those women. But he loved me.

My pride, my ego just got in the way of seeing that.

"Declan Fox is a good person," I say out loud. My voice sounds as stunned as I feel.

It's after four now, and the wind leaking through the window feels even chillier since I'm not under the bed covers. Or maybe it's the fact that I abused and ranted at a perfectly decent human being. That's enough to make me feel chilled.

I suppose, since I'm in Britain, there's only one thing for this self-disillusionment and cold embarrassment.

I'll make myself a cup of tea.

I tiptoe down the creaky stairs and quietly push open the swinging door to the kitchen. When I do, Arya looks up from the kitchen table.

She blinks at me owlishly.

There's a pot of tea, a plate of cheese scones and her journal full of birding sketches on the table.

"Couldn't sleep?" she asks.

I shake my head. "You either?"

She gets up and pulls out a tea cup from the cupboard. "Come on then."

I drop into the old wooden chair and it groans under my weight. I'm not that heavy, it's just a really old chair.

After she's poured me a cup of tea, I blurt out, "It's awful. Declan loves me."

That goes over about as well as I expect. But I tell her about how I was wrong about Declan and also about Michael.

"I knew he was a rat," she says.

And then I tell Arya that Declan heard us at the brunch and her and Kate at the airport and that's why Percy hasn't returned her calls.

Finally, when I'm done, I say, "I'm sorry. I wanted to help you get Percy back. I wanted to help Kate reunite with her family. I wanted to like Michael. I wanted to loathe Declan. It seems that the only thing I've managed to do is make a mess of everything."

I shrug helplessly and take a mournful sip of the bitter, over-steeped black tea.

Arya lets out a high, giddy laugh.

"What?" I ask. I have no idea what's funny about any of this mess.

"I chased a man across the world." She covers her mouth and stifles another laugh.

"Are you alright?"

She snorts and shakes her head. Her eyes sparkle. "Me. The logical, science-based, cool-headed one. The one with the database of fatal flaws and exes, the one who knows that no man is perfect. I chased one of them across the Atlantic." She snorts again and holds back another laugh.

"Well, I mean, I did kind of convince you to come. All that "it's fate" talk."

Her shoulders shake. "He thought I was after his castle. His money. His status." She snorts again.

"More like his birds," I say, gesturing at her sketches.

"I became a fool for him. I've never been a fool."

I have to agree with her. "I was getting concerned. You were wandering around the rocky coastline like one of those creepy gothic widows in their night robes wailing into the wind. It wasn't a good look on you."

She smacks her forehead with the palm of her hand.

"At least you didn't get locked in his attic," I say helpfully.

"That's the plot of *Jane Eyre*," Arya says. She pulls her hand down and I'm glad to see that she's looking happier.

"Will you try and contact him?" I ask.

"Will you contact Declan?" she asks in return.

There's a heavy stone-like feeling in my chest when she says his name. I rub my finger over a tea stain on the wood table and avoid her eyes. This is the question I've been asking myself. The stone lodges into place when I answer her.

"No. He said everything he needed to. We don't need to rehash things."

She raises her eyebrows. "Are you sure? I mean, his only fatal flaw is that he meddles, which some might say is an effort to protect his friends." She looks down at her tea cup, "Well, I mean there are the other flaws of icy demeanor and staring at you too much."

"He doesn't stare too much," I quickly defend him.

Arya grins. "He does. He always stares at you. It's a flaw."

"It's only a flaw if it's unwelcome."

Arya snorts.

I squirm when I realize I just admitted that his staring was welcome.

But then I shake my head and come back to the point. "I don't love him. I only just realized he's not actually awful. I don't want to lead him on. It wouldn't be fair."

Arya shrugs.

"I'll send an email," I say. "I'll tell him I'm sorry for misjudging him. That should give enough closure."

"Mhmm." Arya reaches forward and picks up her art pencil from the table and flips to a blank page in her journal.

"Whatcha doing?" I ask.

She writes out a sentence at the top of the page and underlines it. Then scribbles beneath it. When she's done she flips the journal to me.

"You asked if I was going to contact Percy."

I nod and look down at the journal. It says "Fatal flaw." Beneath that it says, "Doesn't trust me. Breaks my heart."

"Is that worse than clipping your toenails at the table?" I ask.

Arya picks up the journal and smacks me with it. I laugh. Then, I ask, "Will you be alright?"

She sets down the journal and takes a moment to think it over.

Finally she says, "I think Percy was the first man I ever crashed into love with. It takes a bit to recover from that. But I'll be okay. I've got you, don't I? And my boobies."

I chuckle. "Those boobies. They don't know how lucky they are."

"No, I was talking about these beauties." She points at the chest area of her bulky sweater. You can see absolutely nothing beneath the thick wool. Unlike Kate and me, Arya is pretty small in the boob area.

"My mom always said a matchmaker will be able to find me a real gem of man with breasts like mine." She holds her hands in front of her chest. "She always says, "Arya, they're perfect, like two ripe kumquats. Any man will want to squeeze them at night.""

I can't help it, I snort. "You have to be kidding."

She gives me a smile and bats her eyelashes.

"Your mom is sick," I say.

"My mom wants grandchildren."

There's not much to say to that. Arya's mom is notorious for wanting to lasso her with a matchmaker and reel in a groom.

"It'll all work out," I say, even though I'm not sure it will.

Arya shrugs, then looks down at her watch. "Harriet will be up soon."

It's after five and Harriet's an early riser.

A phone chimes and Arya pulls her cell from her pocket.

"It's Kate," she says with a smile. Then she gasps.

"What?" I try to see the screen of her phone.

"She's in England," Arya says.

Whoa. Kate hasn't been back to England since she left on her ill-fated affair with the jet-skier.

"Is she coming to see us? Or her family?"

Arya shakes her head and when she looks up at me my stomach drops. This isn't good.

"She's getting married."

"What?" I scoot back my chair and stand. I look around the kitchen like somehow I'll see Kate in a wedding dress next to the fridge.

"Where? To who?" And just in case Arya missed it the first time, I say, "What?"

Arya looks at me, her eyes wide. "Kate's eloping with Michael."

Michael?

Holy. Freaking. No.

21

KATE DOESN'T ANSWER HER PHONE. OR ANY OF THE FIVE thousand texts we send.

I start with sending "call me" and "what's happening" and "where are you" and "can we see you," and then when she doesn't respond to my texts I descend to, "answer your freaking phone or I will hunt you down and commit friendicide."

When that doesn't get a response I finally text, "Kate. Are you okay?"

There's no response and no read notification.

It looks like Kate's initial long-winded text to Arya sharing the happy news of her whirlwind romance with Michael, her impending elopement, and her soon-to-be triumphant return to her family's bosom is the only message we'll receive.

"Try calling Renee. Maybe she knows something," Arya suggests. She's at the kettle, heating water for another pot of tea.

"Good idea."

It's eleven at night on Mariposa and I'm sure Renee's still at the office. She is.

"What's up? I'm balls deep in research—"

"Michael Sherman is a womanizing sham who is known to scam connected and moneyed women for his own advantage. Kate's run off to elope with him. Do you know where she's getting married? Did she tell you anything about this? We have to stop her."

Renee blows out a long breath. "Hold on. You're telling me, while Kate was busy being an immoral gold digger chasing her white whale, she was caught by an immoral male gold digger with her as his white whale?"

Well, if you put it that way, "Errrm. Yes?"

"She has terrible taste in men. This is the perfect example of karma. If only the legal system worked this way, my job would be so much easier. This is why it's better to love your job, not men."

"So, you don't know anything?"

She doesn't. But she does find a sort of twisted humor in the situation that I fail to grasp.

I hang up and scrub at my eyes. Since I had zero sleep last night they feel like they're being rubbed with gritty sand full of spiky coral and broken glass.

"No luck?" asks Arya.

I shake my head. I've had a few minutes to replay all the interactions I had with Michael and I've come to an unfortunate conclusion.

"I think Michael came to Mariposa specifically for Kate."

Arya frowns at me. "What are you talking about?" She pours steaming black tea into both of our cups. What I wouldn't give for a strong cup of full-bodied, rich, super-caffeinated coffee.

Arya sits across from me and takes a sip of the tea.

"The first time I met Michael, he was watching Kate dance with Declan at the turtle gala."

"So?" Arya says. "Lots of people were watching them. You yourself were staring at Declan."

I wave that aside.

"When I asked how long he'd be staying, he looked at Kate and said that it depended on how his venture panned out."

"I don't know," Arya says. I watch as she dumps three spoons full of sugar into her mug. The spoon clinks against the ceramic as she stirs.

"On the sailboat, he said he'd come to Mariposa after he'd heard about an opportunity that he knew would be profitable. When I asked his business he said mergers and acquisitions. And then he looked at where Kate had been standing."

I remember the moment exactly. I thought he was looking at Declan, but he wasn't. Then I remember him at the beach cleanup. How he and Kate were strolling arm in arm down the beach. After that, Kate stopped coming around for girls' night, she said she'd given up bagging a billionaire, and she'd been busy almost every night.

"He must've heard about Kate. About the heiress in

exile." I finger quote "heiress." Kate comes from a top-tier family, they have connections to the cream of society, they're wealthy, connected...honestly, she's actually the type of woman Declan claimed he usually dated.

Maybe her mom or dad made it known in their circles that if Kate married the right sort she'd be welcomed back into the fold. Which meant she'd be in line to inherit property, money, status. All the things that Declan said Michael chased after.

Arya decides to give up all pretention of sipping her tea. She tips it back and chugs it. Then she sets down the mug and wipes her mouth. I can tell she's come to a conclusion.

"What is it?" I ask. "Do we keep texting, calling? Rent a car? Try to find her? Stop her?"

I remember how Declan said he'd do everything in his power to stop a friend from making a disastrous match. Now I know how he feels.

"In the whole of England?" Arya shakes her head. "I think, knowing Kate, she's probably head over heels in love with Michael."

Oh. Ohhh.

I nod sadly. "Yeah. You're probably right."

"And maybe, in spite of his rat nature, Michael loves her back?"

I stare at Arya in disbelief.

"Or not."

I shake my head. "I need coffee. I really, really need coffee."

22

Harriet decides today is the perfect day for an outing. She's wide awake, chipper and full of energy after a filling breakfast of eggs, black pudding, toast and tomatoes.

"We'll go to Vindolanda and Housesteads and wander along Hadrian's Wall. I'll put together a picnic." Vindolanda and Housesteads are excavations of Roman forts. "There are birds, Arya," Harriet says temptingly.

Arya decides to come. And so we spend the next eight hours tromping around the countryside, climbing up hills, wandering through ancient stone piles, the wind whipping against our cheeks, the blue sky and bright sun trying and failing to warm us. I check my phone every thirty seconds and Arya checks hers every minute.

The late afternoon shadows begin to fall over the walls of the stone fort and I start to fantasize about the cozy down duvet on my creaky bed.

"Dears," Harriet says, after we're piled into her car and heading down the road back toward her home.

"Hmmm?" I say. My eyelids drift down as the sun plays over them in a lullaby pattern flickering through the trees.

"I have one more stop. There's a private estate open to the public one week a year, and today is the final day this year. I've wanted to visit for some time. You don't mind, do you?"

I hear Arya let out a little snore. She's fallen asleep in the back seat.

"No. I don't mind," I say.

"Perfect. I want to poke around to see if I might do a survey of the property. This is a little covert research." She winks at me then looks back at the road.

I laugh at the devious expression on her face. It's at complete odds with her tweed jacket and eccentric researcher persona.

After an hour driving through hedge-lined back roads, past old stone churches, and tiny villages we pull down a long, winding gravel drive. Down the drive, over grassy hills, and centered in the middle of a manicured garden is the epitome of the beautiful, historic, English grand estate. The home sprawls over the green grass, with tall bright windows, a dozen chimneys, and sweeping stairs at the wide entrance. The stone walls glitter like a jewel in the low setting sun. The house looks as if it belongs in a period drama, or a fantasy novel.

"Lovely, isn't it?" Harriet asks.

Her hatchback bumps over the drive.

"Gorgeous," I say.

And I mean it. I'm used to luxurious houses. Kate is a luxury realtor and I've tagged along on many, many house tours. But I've never seen a home that looks like it was pulled out of a fairy tale.

It's beautiful.

There's a hedge maze that's at least an acre, a walled rose garden not yet in bloom, another garden with a trellised entry. Herbs, maybe? Down the hill to the west is a largish blue-watered pond with a wide-limbed, leafy tree leaning over the water.

Harriet pulls to a stop along the side of the house. "Are you ready? The article said the grounds are open to guests. We won't bother with the house."

Arya gives a sleepy moan from the back. "I'll stay here." She unbuckles and drops down to the seat.

I smile at Harriet. We step out of the car and I immediately hear birds singing from the gardens nearby.

"I have a hunch there's something worth seeing at the edge of the property." She points to a grassy, hilly mound about half a mile away.

"Do you mind if I explore the gardens instead?" I ask.

"Not at all."

Harriet heads down the hill and I walk along the path through the rose garden and then under the wood trellis. I was right, it's an herb garden. The scent of lavender greets me. At first, I keep looking back at the house, worried that someone will come out and tell me to leave or ask my business. But, after a few minutes of wandering, I see a gardener digging in the soil. When he notices me, he waves, comments on the weather, and then asks me if I'm enjoying the gardens.

After that, I don't feel uncomfortable exploring.

The sun spills over my back and the birds sing, making me feel relaxed and sleepy. I pull my phone from my pocket. Still nothing from Kate.

I imagine Harriet will be at least another thirty minutes, so I decide to explore the hedge maze. I've always wanted to try one.

The hedges are at least six feet tall, dense green, and spaced about four feet apart. As I walk down the path, I try to watch the location of the sun so that I can steer myself toward the middle of the maze. Finally, after ten minutes of walking I hear a bubbling sound. I follow it and pop out into a small circular area.

It's amazing.

The dark green hedge surrounds the clearing in a curved circular line. There's another opening on the opposite side of the clearing. In the center is a large circular stone fountain. The edge of the fountain is surrounded by a wide bench seat. The center is full of water reflecting the blue sky and clouds floating overhead. In the middle of the water is a life-size statue of a man and a woman. They're holding hands, and from their hands flows a waterfall into the pool. The woman looks down at the water and the man looks at the woman.

I stand and stare for a moment and just listen to the tinkling water and the birds singing. Then I decide to sit down and have a little rest.

I set my phone alarm for twenty minutes and lie down on the bench seat and close my eyes.

The sound of the running water reminds me of Mariposa. My half-asleep mind pulls up images of floating in the bioluminescence. But this time, instead of just touching hands, Declan grabs my hand, pulls me to him and kisses me. I'm too tired to shove the vision away.

"Isla," he says.

I smile and imagine him kissing me more.

"Isla."

He shouldn't be talking. He should be kissing.

"Isla. What are you doing here?"

My eyes fly open and I scramble up on the bench seat.

There's Declan, looming over me, his arms crossed over his chest, the space between his eyebrows pinched.

"Oh. Ah. Oh."

I've lost the power of speech.

I quickly stand up and pat down my clothes and my hair and try to come back to reality.

"Harriet..." I point in a random direction, decide that isn't the way she went and point in another. "Harriet wanted to search for Roman...wait a minute, what are you doing here?"

He lifts his eyebrows, then slowly uncrosses his arms. The stand-offish, suspicious expression on his face fades. "Harriet's poking around?"

I swallow and then nod. Darn it, I'm finally warm again. The sun and all the walking today did nothing, but as soon as I see Declan I'm as toasty as the beach on Mariposa.

"We've been doing the Roman tour today," I say. "It's nice weather for an outing." Ugh. This is awkward. Horribly awkward. Painfully awkward.

"Perfect weather," he agrees.

He puts his hands in his pockets and looks around the clearing.

I break the awkward silence. "Harriet said this place is only open one week a year. She's been wanting to come for some time. It's lovely, don't you think?"

Oh gosh. I've descended into small talk purgatory. The politeness of it stretches painfully between us. Should I just launch into my apology? Tell him I'm sorry for misjudging him?

"You like the estate?" he finally asks.

"I do." I tell him honestly. "Very much. I've never seen such a beautiful home."

His lips twitch into an almost smile.

"Don't even think about buying it," I say. Then I let myself smile at him, which is what I've wanted to do since he barged in on my private little clearing.

His almost smile becomes a full smile.

"Did you...did you receive my email?" he asks.

I nod. But the mention of his email reminds me of Kate, and all my worries and fears for her.

"I'm sorry," I begin. I bite my lip, remembering all that I said to him. That I don't like him.

But I do like him. I do.

I may not love him, but I like him.

My phone lets out the chime that's unique to Kate.

She's finally texted. I hold up my hand, "I'm sorry. Don't leave, I just have to check this."

I pull my phone out of my pocket and read her text.

Oh no.

Declan steps toward me. "Are you alright? You look..."

I glance up at him. What is Kate doing?

"You should sit down," he says.

Apparently, Kate's text made me look like garbage. I shake my head. "It's not...it's Kate. She texted this morning." I hold up my phone. "Michael convinced her to elope. I think...I think he sought her out and preyed upon her desire to reunite with her family. She has the connections he wants, the status. I don't know where she is. Somewhere in England." I look at Declan with the helplessness and shame that I feel. "I don't know if she's already married or..."

I look down and squeeze my eyes together. I feel so angry and so helpless that there are tears burning at the back of my eyes. Kate's my best friend, she's gone off with a known skeeve, and I don't know how to help her.

"I finally understand how you felt when you thought Arya was a schemer and..."

When I look up, Declan has lost his relaxed posture. He's closed off and cold again.

His closed expression hurts me more than it should.

"I'm sorry," I say, shaking my head. "I didn't mean to involve you in this. I just...I don't know what to do."

Declan gives a sharp nod. Then gestures toward the hedge maze. "I believe the estate closes to guests at five."

I stare at him for a moment, not exactly

comprehending what he's saying. Then it dawns on me. He doesn't want anything to do with me anymore. Not me. Not Kate. Not Arya. Not Michael. Not any of us.

Why would he, when I blatantly told him that nothing would ever entice me to date him, marry him, love him or even like him?

He finds the way out of the maze much faster than I came in. We're back at the entrance in less than two horribly silent minutes.

I thought yesterday was goodbye. That was bad enough. This is even worse.

I pause when we're at the entrance to the hedge maze. Declan stops with me, but he looks distracted and impatient to be gone.

"For what it's worth," I begin.

Then in the distance I hear a sharp, "Helloooo. Isla. Helloooo." I look toward the house. Harriet flaps her arms at me from the car. "Helloooo. Time to go."

"I suppose it's another goodbye," Declan says stiffly. He nods to me.

"Helloooo." Harriet calls again.

I look toward Harriet and then back at Declan. I'd like to say a hundred things to him, but I have no idea how.

You make me tingly and warm. I want to eat apricots when I'm around you. You remind me of sunburn and wool sweaters. I like it when you smile. Thank you for jumping into the water after me. Thank you for letting me sleep on your chest. Maybe...maybe you'd like to come and help paint a room in my cottage? Or take a walk on the beach?

"For what it's worth," I begin again.

Declan reaches out and takes my hand. His grip is firm and impersonal.

"Take care of yourself," he says.

Then he drops my hand and turns and strides quickly toward the carpark.

I stare after him, completely stunned.

His hand.

His touch.

His...

Oh my word.

"It's happened," I say.

I stare at my hand. It's tingly and warm and I can still feel the lingering touch of Declan's fingers brushing over mine. The warmth travels up my arm and over my whole body until I feel like I'm floating in the bioluminescence, surrounded by glowing lights.

Oh my word.

It's that moment. That moment when you realize the person that you thought you disliked, you actually like, that the person you thought you liked, you actually love.

I *love* Declan Fox.

"Oh no. Oh no."

I have the worst timing. The worst. My horrible, meandering slow boat trip to love arrived after the train already left the station.

I told him I'd never love him, and a day later, I realize that I do. That I probably have for quite some time. It snuck up on me, like the color of the sea shifting from aqua to navy blue. You don't know the exact moment the color changes, only that it does.

I love Declan Fox.

"Helloooo. Isla. Time to go." Harriet waves her arms at me.

I close my eyes, let out a long, slow breath and then decide that the only thing I can do is keep moving on.

When I get to the car Harriet says, "Was that Declan Fox?"

I nod. I suppose he has a distinct enough look that he's hard to mistake for anyone else.

"Did you ask him about surveying for a Roman fort?"

I shake my head. "Why would I ask him that?"

Harriet frowns at me, and her hair blows ferociously around her head, adding to her irritated expression. "Because he owns this estate. Who else would you ask?"

My heart feels like it drops out of my chest and hits the gravel.

Declan owns this estate? He owns the most beautiful house I've ever seen? Declan?

No wonder he smiled.

I press my hand to my stomach when I realize the implications. If I tell Declan tomorrow, or even a week from now, that I've changed my mind and suddenly realized I love him, what will he think?

He'll think the only logical thing.

That I've been swayed by his estate, his wealth...that I'm exactly what he first believed. A gold digger.

No wonder he left in such a hurry.

I would've run too.

There's no way he could think that my being here was a coincidence. No, it was just me, checking out the prospects.

Seeing what he had to offer.

I climb into the car.

Arya sits up. "Have a good time?"

"It was great," I say woodenly.

The knowledge of love is heavy and uncomfortable. No wonder Arya turned into a tragic gothic heroine. Love feels awful.

I look down at my hand and run my fingers over where Declan touched me.

The entire ride home Harriet regales us with stories of university politics.

I nod, make innocuous comments, and torture myself with thoughts of what could have been.

23

THE NEXT TWO DAYS PASS QUICKLY. HARRIET'S IN A FLURRY of activity, trying to relay another decade of research before I leave. We work eighteen-hour days and I barely have any time at all to think about could have beens or would have beens.

When we got back from Declan's estate I wrestled with myself over whether or not to send him an email. The coldness of his expression, the way he said goodbye, and what he might think of me all swayed me toward not emailing. But the way he told me that he believed in love at first sight swayed me toward emailing.

There's a saying my grandma had, "If you keep waiting for the perfect conditions to plant, you'll never have a garden."

I decided to write.

I sent him a short note, it said, "I'm sorry for what I

said the other day. I misjudged you. If I could take my words back, I would. I do like you. Very much."

I left it at that. I hit the send button on sheer nerve before I could chicken out and erase everything.

He hasn't replied.

It's lunch now, nearly forty-eight hours since I last saw him. We're leaving England tomorrow.

Arya has a notebook opened next to her plate. "Did you know that puffins breed for life?" She draws a curved bill on the puffin she's sketching. To me, it looks a mix between a parrot and a penguin.

"Huh. Just like the booby," I say.

I take a bite of my ploughman's sandwich. The cheddar is tangy and the pickle has a nice bite.

Harriet made them for us before heading out to the shops on a chocolate and tea run.

"I'll be happy to get home," Arya says. She drops her pencil and gives me a wry smile. "Not that there weren't plenty of birds to keep me occupied. Ever since Percy mentioned the Farne Islands and all the puffins I wanted to come."

I reach over and squeeze her arm.

She shrugs. "Don't worry about me."

"I won't." To lighten the mood I say, "You've got your kumquats."

She snorts and then after a minute she frowns down at her half-eaten sandwich. "What do you think Kate's doing?"

"I don't know," I say. "But when I see her I'm going to—"

The doorbell rings.

I lean back in my chair and look from the solarium to the front of the house. In the front window I see an Italian sports car in the drive and Michael and Kate on the stoop.

The front legs of my chair smack back to the ground. I'm stunned and jarred. Kate's here. I shove my chair back and jump up.

"It's Kate."

"What?" Arya hops up and runs toward the front door.

"And Michael," I call after her.

My stomach feels queasy as I hurry out of the solarium. Are they married? Do I have time to tell her the truth about Michael?

I get to the front right when Arya swings open the door. I stop short. Michael has his arm around Kate and she's snuggled into his side. He has a bashful, amicable, aww shucks sort of look on his face. Kate looks deliriously happy. Yes. That happy.

At her look I readjust everything I was about to say.

"Kate!" Arya rushes forward and throws her arms around Kate. She pulls her away from Michael and hugs her tight. While Arya hugs her and Kate laughs, Michael and I look at each other.

That look tells me everything I need to know.

He's a smiling, amiable, friendly rat. And he knows it.

He strides over to me and takes my hand. "We were friends before, now that I've married your best friend, I hope we can be even better friends."

My stomach sinks. That's it then. They've married.

I never noticed it before, but his charm, the careful

sweep of his walnut-colored hair, his casual yet still cultured clothing, everything about him is perfectly suited to putting people at ease.

It worked on me. I completely fell for the outward appearance he presented and missed everything happening beneath the surface.

"Perhaps," I say to him. I pull my hand away and step back.

Michael's eyebrows lower and he gives a slight frown, as if my less than warm reception is unexpected.

Before he can respond Kate rushes over.

"La-La!" She pulls me into a hug.

I squeeze her and say, "You're happy?"

She pulls back from me and I get a good look at her. She's in an elegant ice-blue lace dress, her hair is glossy and flowing, and her cheeks are pink. She looks radiant. Like a new bride.

"Happier than I've been in years," she says.

Then she loops her arm through mine and says, "Do you have any coffee here? I'm dying for a cup."

Arya snorts and then covers her mouth with her hand.

We make a pot of tea in the kitchen and I pull out a tin of chocolate biscuits and chocolate and orange teacakes. Michael regales us with the story of their elopement.

"When I saw Kate at the gala, my heart was hers," he says, making moon-eyes at Kate. "I knew a woman like her could have any man. A prince, a billionaire, a celebrity, there was no reason for her to choose me above all others."

Arya leans over and whispers, "Suave, isn't he?"

I nod and then carry the teapot over to the kitchen table.

"Michael is friends with my brother," Kate says. She leans into him and he squeezes her close. "He played golf with my father, not three months ago."

Ah. So that's how he heard about Kate. I give them both a bright smile and go to retrieve the biscuits and cake.

"That's quite fortunate," I say.

Arya turns away from Michael and Kate and gives me a pointed look.

We sit around the table. I pour myself a huge cup of tea and grab three biscuits.

"After you fell off the sailboat, Kate and I became closer. Shortly after the beach cleanup I was able to convince her to elope."

Arya's eyebrows raise in surprise.

"That long ago?" I say.

That means for the whole month that Kate was distracted and missing girls' nights she was actually with Michael. While I was going out on lunch dates with him he was dating my best friend.

Kate looks down at the milky tea in her cup, then back up at me.

"A twenty-nine days' notice at the registrar is required to marry. We married as soon as our twenty-nine days were up," says Michael. Then he kisses Kate on the check and says, "They were the longest twenty-nine days of my life."

I'll bet they were.

I stand up. "Can I speak to you?" I ask Kate. I nod toward the hallway. "Privately?"

She nods and stands.

"Don't be long," Michael says. He gives her another kiss.

I try not to let my distaste show. I hurry down the hall, through the solarium and into the back garden. When the door shuts I turn back to Kate.

The cottage garden's spring flowers bloom in pastel pink, Easter blue and light yellow. The green foliage and stone wall provide a bit of privacy.

"I know what you're going to say," Kate says, before I can start in on her.

I shake my head. "I don't think you do."

She looks up at the weak blue sky and then back at me. Her gaze is steady and clear. The deliriously happy look that I saw earlier is gone. I take a step forward.

"Kate..."

I stop.

What exactly do I want to say?

Your husband is a sleaze? He married you out of avarice? Why did you lie to me for a whole month? What have you done?

No.

When I was younger my mom would always say something to my dad when I didn't do what he wanted. She'd say, "Dearest, everyone has the right to go to hell in a hand-basket of their own making." Which always meant, leave the poor girl alone, she can make her own choices.

Even if I messed up, or chose wrong, I liked that my mom gave me the choice to do so.

I reach out and take Kate's hands. They're cold, so I

give them a squeeze. I'm in my oversized sweater and pants, but Kate's in her tiny dress.

"Come here you," I say. I lead her down the little cobblestone path to a stone bench and then pull her down next to me. I wrap an arm around her shoulder. "So, you're married to Michael."

She drops her head to my shoulder.

"I didn't see that one coming," I say.

She half-hiccups, half-laughs.

"Do you love him?" I ask.

"No," she says simply.

So Arya was wrong, Kate wasn't head over heels in love.

I nod. Then I ask, "Does he love you?"

"Probably not."

I let out a long sigh. I lean my head against hers. What a pickle. I look up at the pale blue of the sky and the clouds flying swiftly past. A bird starts to chirp as it hops across the short garden grass.

"Not every marriage needs to be built on love," she says.

"It's a good start."

"But not the only start." She sits up straight and faces me. "La-La, I know you fancied Michael."

I shake my head. "It's not that—"

She gives me a disbelieving look. "But you and he would never have worked."

"I know." I have no arguments against that.

Kate puts on her realtor look, where she's about to list off all the important details of a property.

"I married Michael because he has the right connections. He went to Cambridge, he runs with the right set. My mum told me my father approves of him. La-La, I'll be seeing my family tonight for the first time in five years. *Five years.* Michael wants my connections. I want my family back. We both win."

I frown. "You knew? He actually told you he wanted to marry you for your family status?"

Apparently the shock is clear in my voice because Kate smirks at me and I see that bold irreverence that I've always loved in her.

"At first he tried the lovestruck routine on me, all adoring and charming. You're beautiful, you're the sun in my sky, garbage like that." She snorts. "Michael's golden charm may have fooled you, but I'm not like you."

"What's that supposed to mean?"

She nudges her elbow into my side. "Just that you take people based on what they present, not on what they keep hidden."

I frown. That's exactly the conclusion I came to recently.

She shrugs. "If someone acts like a good person, you think they are. I'm not like that. Probably because I act like a good person most of the time, but I'm not really all that good on the inside. Not really."

"You are."

She shakes her head. "La-La, I married the man my best friend was dating. A man she had set her hopes on. Does a good person do that?"

I see her point. But... "I still choose to think of you as a good person."

Kate smiles. "That's because you're incredibly loyal. And the best friend I have."

I nod and drop my elbows to me knees. I lean forward and stare at the little cluster of blooming candy pink hyacinth. They seem a little too happy for this conversation.

"Did you at least get a prenup?" I ask, thinking of Renee's advice.

"What do you take me for?" Kate asks. I look over at her and she smirks. "Ironclad. I'll come out of this smelling like roses."

"What does Michael get then?" I ask, wondering how she convinced him to sign away his rights to any proceeds from a divorce.

"Great sex," she says.

I fake gag and she laughs.

"Seriously," I say.

She lifts an eyebrow. "He gets my family connections, he gets to give away half of his wealth in our eventual divorce and he gets a first wife. Everything a man of substance could ever desire. Remember? Men love this sort of thing."

"I thought you were joking when you mentioned this before. When you were aiming for Declan."

"That's because you thought I was good."

"You are good," I say.

She doesn't respond. We both stare toward the

windows of the solarium reflecting the soft spring sun. I think we'll have to go in soon.

"Are you going to live in England?"

"Yes," she says simply. Then she turns to me with that deliriously happy smile on her face again. "I get to see my niece and nephew. I'll be in my sister's wedding. I can have my mum's pudding. I can go *home*. All that, La-La, and all I had to do was marry a charming, good-looking gold digger."

"There's a great deal of irony in there," I say wryly.

She stands up and brushes off her skirt. I stand too and we make our way back to the house.

"Speaking of irony, Declan Fox was the best man at my wedding."

My stomach does a hard flip. "What did you say?" I stop walking.

Kate turns around and gives me a conspiratorial smile. "I know. It was ridiculous. He showed up out of nowhere at our hotel and strong-armed Michael into signing the prenup. I wasn't sure he would until Declan arrived." She shrugs. "Then he stood as best man at our wedding. It was just the three of us. Very awkward. He didn't say a word. I swear that man has a stick up his arse a mile long. Since I married without love, I'm glad I chose Michael and not Declan. You were right, La-La, that man is arrogant and cold. I don't know where he gets off ordering people about like he does. I would've hated being his wife. Even if it was only for a year."

I'm having a hard time taking in what Kate's saying.

Declan was at her wedding. He found them and made certain that Kate was protected.

"Did Declan say anything? About why he came?"

Kate shakes her head. "He left right after the ceremony. Didn't say anything at all. Not even congratulations." She looks put out about that and I almost laugh. Although it'd be a hysterical sort of laugh.

Instead I pull open the door to the solarium and follow Kate back inside. I can hear Arya and Michael talking in the kitchen. Before we go back I catch Kate by the arm.

"I'll miss you," I say.

She nods and I see the beginning of tears in her eyes. "Don't worry. I'll be back in a year or two."

After the divorce, I suppose she means.

"Maybe not. Maybe you'll fall in love and live happily ever after."

She thinks about that for a moment then says, "I think my happily ever after and your happily ever after are two different destinations."

I study her expression. Then I say, "I think you're right."

When we walk back to the kitchen I see that Harriet is back from the shops. She's brought out a bottle of champagne and more teacakes.

"It's the bride," she says happily when she sees us. "Congratulations! You must be Kate."

At that she pops the cork.

Arya sends me a look, which I know means, how could you leave me with the rat for so long.

"Sorry," I mouth at her.

She shakes her head and grabs a champagne glass.

After a round of toasts for good health, good fortune, a good marriage, and a good life, we clink our glasses and drink.

"Young love," Harriet says. "Isn't it lovely?"

Apparently Michael has been sharing his stories with Harriet.

I take a long gulp of the champagne. The bubbles sting my throat as they go down. While Arya talks with Kate and Harriet dishes up teacakes, Michael wanders over to my side. I try not to stiffen at his approach.

He holds out his glass and clinks mine. "I'm pleased to see you again."

I think he'd like me to absolve him for leading me astray. I assume he was only using me to get closer to Kate, or perhaps to make Declan jealous. I don't know which, maybe both.

His eyes are friendly and guileless. I think Kate was right, I see people as I want to see them. Michael seems to be the epitome of kindness and sincerity.

I smile at him, then say, "Kate told me Declan was at your wedding."

The change that comes over Michael is subtle but immediate. His friendly expression turns wary.

"Yes." I can see the flurry of thoughts taking place behind his eyes. "Dec and I have decided to leave the past behind us."

Meaning I should too.

Then something occurs to me. It's either the guilty look on Michael's face or the way he says the words, but I suddenly remember Kate saying that she didn't think Michael was going to sign the prenup until Declan showed up.

"Did Declan give you something?" I ask. That doesn't come out right, but Michael gets the point. Sort of.

He leans closer to me, giving me that look like he's about to share a confidence. He touches his nose, telling me this is a secret. "Dec finally gave me the money I deserved from my father's estate. A wedding gift of sorts."

My eyes open wide and Michael nods.

"I know. Dec's arrogance knows no bounds. You and I both know that." He winks at me.

I give him a weak smile. He still thinks I don't care for Declan. That I find him arrogant and cold. That I want nothing to do with him.

Michael clinks his glass against mine. "I'm glad we had this talk. I expect we'll stay friends for a long time."

He smiles at me and I smile back, although my stomach churns uncomfortably.

Declan...

When Declan left me at the edge of the maze, he wasn't hurrying to get away from me, he was hurrying to help me. To help my friend.

How many times have I gotten him wrong? How many times do I have to correct myself before I learn to trust that despite his outward demeanor he's a good person. A kind person.

Declan made sure Kate was okay.

He gave Michael money he didn't deserve. It seems like he kept the truth from Michael about how poorly his father behaved – to keep Michael's positive memories of his father from being tarnished. All this, because I looked upset and told Declan how worried I was.

Does that mean...?

Does he still care for me?

My breath feels short and tight in my lungs.

Michael frowns at me, he looks as if he's waiting for my response to something.

"I'm sorry. What did you say?"

"I asked if you'll be returning to Mariposa soon. Swim with the turtles and all that."

"Yes, of course," I say distractedly. But then something else occurs to me. "Michael, if you loved Kate from the time you saw her at the gala, then why did you send me the turtle?"

Michael gives me a confused smile. "What turtle?"

"The turtle sculpture. From the gala," I say. The one he sent with the note that said, *Look, a turtle. It's pretty but you're prettier.* It was the reason I invited him on the sail.

Michael shakes his head. "I'm sorry. I don't remember a turtle. Was it something important?"

I stare at him. He's honestly confused. He has no idea what I'm talking about. Which can only mean one thing. He didn't send it.

"No. It wasn't important. Never mind."

He nods and then excuses himself to go sit by Kate.

I stare out the kitchen window. Thinking and thinking and trying to come to any conclusion but the one I know is the right one.

Declan sent the turtle.

Even the phrase, *look, a turtle,* was a clue. It's what I said when we were kayaking. Look, a sea turtle.

If I'd paid the least bit of attention, I'd have realized it was him. I would've realized he cared.

For the next hour I keep up the conversation with Kate, Michael, Arya and Harriet. I laugh at the stories, I drink to more toasts, I wish Kate and Michael well, I give lots of hugs. The whole while my chest pinches tight and my mind keeps repeating, does he still care for me, does he, does he?

After Kate and Michael leave I tell Harriet I need a moment before we can get back to work, then I rush up the stairs to my bedroom.

I sit on the creaky bed and pull open my email.

There's nothing. No response to the email I sent days ago.

I open a new message and type another email. This one says, "Declan. I saw Kate and Michael today. Thank you. I don't know if you did it for me, but thank you. I don't know what to think. I only know that I wish I could thank you in person. Would you please come see me tomorrow at Harriet's? We're leaving the next day for home. I want to see you before I go. Please write back. Writing back is like saying goodbye, it's necessary, do I have to teach you how to do that too? Or don't write back, just come so I can thank you. Isla."

I hold my breath when I push send, then I hold it a bit longer for luck. I metaphorically hold my breath the rest of the day, and then the next. And I don't stop until Harriet has waved goodbye, Arya and I have dropped our bags at the airline counter, and we're boarding the airplane for Mariposa.

He didn't write back.

He didn't come to say goodbye or to get thanks.

The hope that he'll come running into the airport and stop me with a kiss like a hero in some 1990s romcom fades.

He doesn't come.

He doesn't write.

This is real life, not a movie.

And in real life hearts get broken all the time.

24

FOR THE FIRST TIME IN A DECADE I STAY AWAKE FOR A PLANE ride. It's uncomfortable. But not because of overwhelming fear or flying phobia. No. It's uncomfortable because I'm facing the fact that I've made a mess of things.

I was so prejudiced against Declan, from the very start, that I couldn't see past my own pride.

I stare out the airplane window at the blue, blue sky and the clouds far below. A month ago, I thought I knew exactly what I wanted in life. To write articles for the paper, to renovate my cottage, and to maybe someday slowly and quietly fall into love with a nice, easy sort of man.

Someone like Michael.

Or Theo.

I cringe at the thought.

Declan said that I wasn't at all like the women he usually dated, that he would never have chosen me for himself. It made me angry at the time. But now, I realize he isn't like the men I chose either. The men I chose had the appearance of goodness but were never actually good in truth.

I suppose my heart knew better than my mind.

The flight attendant wheels the cart by and asks Arya and me if we'd like any tea or coffee.

"Tea please," I say.

Arya shakes her head and closes her eyes. She doesn't seem worried or anxious like she did on the plane ride to England. In fact, she seems resigned. Happy to be heading home, but also resigned.

The flight attendant hands me a full teacup and a packet of shortbread. I take a sip of the steaming hot bitter tea.

Arya opens her eyes and turns to me. "Do you think Kate will be happy?" she asks.

I think about it for a moment. For the last five years, the one thing Kate wanted most was to go home. To be welcomed back by her family. With Michael she finally achieved her wish.

I give Arya a small smile. "I don't know. I hope so."

She nods. "Me too."

Arya closes her eyes again, and soon she's asleep. I have to admit the low hum of the jet engines and the soft vibration of the airplane is rather soothing.

All these years I've been terrified of flying, and the only thing I needed to cure my fear was first, a loathing of Declan Fox, and second, a love for him.

The plane gives a hard bump and my seat shakes. It

gives another jerk and the tea on my tray back sloshes out of the cup. What's happening? I look around the plane but no one seems concerned. My mouth goes dry and my heart pounds. I grasp my armrests and my knuckles turn white. Never mind, love can't cure a fear of flying.

I think about telling Declan about this moment. "Were you afraid?" he'd ask. "Not at all," I'd say. And then he'd grin at me because he'd know I was lying.

I stare out the window, the clouds have cleared and the ocean is far, far below. My mind starts the "Declan tape" again, replaying all our interactions from the moment we met. This time, I let it.

When we land, it's eight at night and dark out. It feels like two in the morning. I can barely keep my eyes open. I hug Arya goodnight, make it home and then fall into bed.

I don't dream.

When the shrill ringing of my cellphone wakes me up, I'm surprised to see bright afternoon light shining through my bedroom window.

"'Lo?" I croak into the receiver.

"Isla. Weren't you awake yet?" It's my mom. She's chiding me, like all moms do when they think you've slept too long and wasted away the day.

"Mom. I'm jetlagged," I say. I sit up in bed and rub at my eyes. "What time is it?"

"In Greece it's seven at night. It's already lunchtime on Mariposa."

"You're in Greece? When did you get there?" I thought she was in Mongolia. I yawn and nearly crack my jaw with how wide my mouth goes.

"No, no. Your father and I met in Greece for a vacation. He finished his assignment in Afghanistan. Do you remember that little inn on the coast in Santorini? We met there."

"Ah," I say.

I'm starting to wake up and I'm back on familiar ground. My parents jumping from country to country and meeting in random locations is the story of my life. And happily, I was usually in this same cottage for all of it. I'm so grateful my mom was wise enough to give me a home full of so much love.

"How long are you in Santorini for?" I ask.

"Never mind that," she says, and I hear the impatience in her voice. "Your father wants to talk to you."

I climb off my bed and stand. "He does?"

He doesn't ever ask to talk to me. Usually my mom forces the phone on him. We've never had much to talk about after I told him point blank I wouldn't be following in his footsteps.

"Here he is," my mom says.

I hear the rustling of the phone and then the silence as my dad takes the phone.

"Isla?" he says. His voice is sharp and deep.

"Hi Dad." I walk across my creaky floor out of my bedroom.

He clears his throat. I wait for him to say whatever it is he needs to. The silence lasts for fifteen seconds. I make it to my living room. The cottage is empty and quiet.

Suddenly, the happiness and love I've always felt here seems less bright. I frown. It almost feels...lonely.

I look toward the kitchen, as if I expect, well, as if I expect Declan to be leaning against the wall, smirking at me. Tossing an apricot in his hand.

I shake my head. The image of Declan disappears.

No, it's just me here. Me and no one else.

Maybe I should ask my parents to come for a visit.

"Was there something you needed?" I ask my dad.

He clears his throat again. "Darn right there is."

I head to the kitchen. Whatever it is, this needs coffee.

"Isla, I'm not good at this sort of thing."

"Mhmm," I say. For a correspondent, my dad is surprisingly terrible at communicating.

"Isla, I was shot."

"What?" I stumble and grab the kitchen wall. The kitchen tilts and sways as I push down my panic.

"Where? When? Are you okay? What happened? Should I come?" The words tumble out of me. My dad was shot and no one told me? Why didn't I hear about this?

"What happened?" I say again.

I realize that I'm clenching the wall so tightly my nails are gouging into the paint. I carefully pull my hand away.

"No, no," he says gruffly. "I'm fine. It was a flesh wound. Nothing serious."

I close my eyes. I readjust the picture I had of my dad bleeding out in a war zone, to a barely bleeding graze.

"Dad. Why didn't you call me? Why didn't Mom?"

The feeling of aloneness deepens. While I was in Britain, worried about Kate, and Arya and everything else, my dad was shot.

"I told her not to," my dad says. "That's why I called."

"Okay," I say. My voice is small. I walk to the table, pull out a chair and drop down.

He clears his throat again, then says, "When I was shot, before I realized it was nothing, only one thought was in my mind." He pauses, and it suddenly occurs to me that my dad might be struggling not to cry.

"What was it?" I ask, although I'm almost afraid to hear.

The wooden chair digs uncomfortably into my legs as I wait for his answer.

Finally, he says, "I was sorry that I wouldn't ever be able to tell you how proud I am of you."

His voice cracks at the end. My mouth quivers and my throat goes tight. I never realized how much I've wanted to hear him say that until just this moment. I can't respond. My throat feels too raw.

"Isla?" He pauses.

"Yes," I whisper.

"I'm proud of you. I never needed you to be like me. I only needed you to be you. It may have appeared otherwise, but I always hoped you knew how I felt."

I stare down at the wood grains of the table. My dad has always been...proud.

And I never, ever knew it.

I took his outside demeanor, his lack of words, as evidence that he didn't approve of me. All along, the opposite was true.

"You're proud of me?"

"Of course I am," he says, and I hear the warmth in his voice. "Ever since you were a toddler, climbing coconut trees and swimming in deep water, you've gone your own way. How could I expect you to follow my path when you've always made your own?"

I close my eyes and hold my breath so that my dad can't hear me crying over the phone. All these years I thought he didn't approve. And he did. He does.

I wipe at my eyes with the back of my hand. Then I clear my throat and say, "Dad?"

"Yes, Isla?"

"Try not to get shot again, okay?"

He laughs, loud and long. I smile at the richness of the sound.

"I'll do my best," he says.

He hands the phone back to my mom, and she asks me all sorts of questions about England, and Harriet, and my plans for the biography. We talk for another fifteen minutes until I yawn so loudly she hears it over the phone.

"Go on, now," she says. "Have some coffee. Your father and I are going to the beach. He's displaying some unique mating rituals, I believe they must be coming from his pseudo-near-near death experience. For example, the other night—"

"Mom," I say.

"Yes?"

"I don't want to know."

"Right. I forgot. You're not an objective researcher."

"Not at all."

She pauses, but she can't hold it in, "Regardless, dear, if a man ever pulls you down a beach in the moonlight and drops you to the sand—"

"Mom."

"Yes, dear?"

"I don't want to know."

I can practically hear her smiling over the phone. I tell her goodbye and she hangs up, to go do whatever she and my dad are about to do at the beach.

For a few minutes, I just sit in the kitchen and stare out the window.

I wonder if I'd ever asked my dad how he felt, if he would've told me? Probably. Instead, I let our relationship rest on assumptions.

Sort of like I did with Declan.

I wonder what would've happened if I'd just asked Declan how he felt? I wonder if I would've been courageous enough to be open to his answer.

I sigh then walk to the living room and pull the sea turtle sculpture off the bookshelf.

My dad's proud of me.

My mom loves me.

I have my job.

A biography to write.

My friends.

My cottage and my garden.

I feel the weight of the turtle in my hand. Why does all that make me feel so lonely?

25

I MAKE MYSELF THE LARGEST POT OF JAMAICAN BLUE Mountain coffee the world has ever seen and then I get busy. My first order of business is to get rid of the cardboard box full of Theo's stuff. I throw it into the trash. It hits the bottom of the can with a satisfying thud. I really don't want to be tethered down anymore by assumptions and judgments and prejudices.

In fact, my own inaction and pre-judgments over the last few years, and especially over the last month, have left me worse for wear. It's time to fix that.

So, I pour myself another full mug of steaming black coffee, sit at the kitchen table and open my laptop. Then I start a brand new lifestyle article.

I'm tired of assumptions, and unasked questions, and misjudgments. That way of living hasn't worked out for me. Instead, I'm going to be direct and forthright and as honest as I can, and see what happens. I made a mistake, and I want to try my best to remedy it.

That's all anyone can do. If you make a mistake, admit it, and then try your best to fix it.

I begin to type.

THREE HOURS LATER I HAVE AN ARTICLE.

I also have two friends banging on my front door.

I ignore them and hit send on my article.

"Isla, hurry up. It's the butterflies."

I restrain a smile.

That's Arya, she always goes bonkers on the first day of butterfly season. And apparently, that's today.

We never know when it's going to arrive, which makes it even better when it happens. Usually it's in March or April. Years ago, we started the tradition of dropping whatever we were doing and getting together to watch the butterflies flit about. Kate always said it's like standing in the middle of a snowstorm. I always thought it was like being inside a snow globe with thousands of butterflies floating around you. Sometimes they fly so close you can feel the beat of their wings kissing your face. It's magical. It's also why the Spanish explorers that discovered our island called it Mariposa. The butterflies were here hundreds of years ago too.

The banging on my front door continues.

"Come on, Isla. I know you're in there. Don't make me come get you." That's Renee. Obviously.

I shut my laptop and look down at my outfit. Jean shorts, pink tank top, flip flops — good enough.

I hurry to my living room and swing open the front door.

It's a little past three, the sky is bright denim blue and a gentle breeze tugs at my hair. The perfect day for butterflies. Still, I scowl at my friends.

"You couldn't text?"

Arya's eyes are bright and she's bouncing up and down on her toes. "No, I couldn't text. Are you crazy? Come on. My boss spotted thousands of them at the preserve. It's like Christmas."

I glance at Renee and raise an eyebrow. "Are you seeing this?"

Renee smirks, "Kids these days."

But I can tell she's as excited as Arya, she just does a better job of holding in her enthusiasm.

"You took off work?" I ask Renee.

She scoffs and then brushes off her black business suit. "It's my one personal day a year. Darn straight I took off work."

I grin at them both. Then, because I'm just as excited as they are, I squeal and start to hop up and down.

Arya drives like a maniac toward the preserve.

"I'm so glad this didn't happen while we were in England," she says.

"I'm so glad you didn't run off with Percy," Renee says. "Then it would've been just me and Isla with the butterflies." She winks at me, so I stick my tongue out at her.

"I wouldn't have. I'm over Percy. Completely, totally, one hundred percent over...Percy?" Arya's voice rises in shock.

We're at the nature preserve.

And sure enough, a slightly sunburned, hopeful-looking Percy is looking toward Arya's car.

"Darn," Renee says. "He actually came back."

Arya pulls to a stop. She glances at me with wide eyes and lets out a stunned breath.

"You're not over him," I say.

"Not even a little," she whispers.

Percy hesitantly holds up a hand toward Arya. A small, questioning wave.

Arya grips the steering wheel. "What if he leaves again?"

Renee snorts. "Arya. Boobies mate for life."

I stifle a laugh.

Arya gives us a smile that reminds me of how happy she is when she sees the butterflies, only more. Much more.

"Go on then," I say.

She nods and then she's racing out of the car. A few feet from Percy she slows to a stop.

All of a sudden Percy grabs Arya, and he's hugging her, and kissing her and then...

"Wow," Renee says.

"That's a big ring," I say.

Percy's down on his knees.

We can see the glint of the ring thirty feet away.

"Do you think she'll say yes?" Renee asks.

I laugh.

Arya pulls Percy up from his knees and they're kissing and... "I don't think we should be watching this," I say.

"Agreed."

We turn aside and look out the window toward the edge of the preserve.

"I wonder what made Percy come back," Renee says.

I look out over the tall grass bowing in the breeze. It's green like the grass in England and green like Declan's eyes when he's happy.

"I do too," I say.

I do too.

26

WE DON'T SEE THE FIELD OF BUTTERFLIES. INSTEAD, RENEE decides to head back to the office. "Work is love" she says. I take the island circuit, a sandy path that follows the coastline, and head toward home.

It's only about two miles from the nature preserve to my cottage and the walk has a beautiful view of the sea. Along the path a few small white butterflies flit along in pairs. Instead of making me glad like it usually does, it makes me feel alone.

The sun dips lower in the sky. In an hour, maybe less, it will start painting the sea in sunset colors.

Suddenly, I have the strongest wish that Declan were here. This would be the moment I told him about. When two people sit on the beach at sunset and brush hands and then...they know.

A few butterflies drift past me.

I close my eyes and make that wish.

When I open them again I look around the beach, somehow expecting that he'll be here.

He's not.

I turn my back on the water and walk up the hill to my cottage. The sunlight filters across the trees in a soft, fuzzy blue.

The sea grape and whistling pines along my road open up and I see the white paint of my little cottage and the turquoise trim of my porch.

And there, sitting on the steps of my porch, is Declan.

A happy, glowing warmth fills me. An answering smile grows on my face. *He's here. He came.*

When Declan sees me he stands. He doesn't smile.

In fact, he looks as cold and stand-offish as ever.

The golden glow of the setting sun shines off his black hair and paints him as stiff and unyielding as a statue.

If I'd seen him like this before, I would've thought that he didn't care. Or that he was horrible or awful. Now...I run.

I run until I'm standing in front of him.

I want to throw my arms around him. I want to tell him all those things I didn't know how to say before but now I do. But instead, I say, "You didn't write me back."

His mouth moves into an almost smile, and I see that his eyes are a happy, grassy green.

I cross my arms to keep from throwing them around him. "When someone emails you that they want you to come say goodbye, you should write them back."

Then, my heart flips over, because he finally does

smile. "I was in France. Admitting to Percy that I'd been wrong."

"Oh," I say. "Thank you."

He gives a short nod.

I uncross my arms and take a step closer to him. "You still could've written though."

He looks at my mouth, and I see in his gaze the same hunger that I'm feeling. My skin starts to itch, like a sunburn after a day on the beach, like the wool of a cozy, English sweater.

He shakes his head no.

"No?" I ask.

"No. I thought, if I had to say anything, I'd rather it be in person."

"Ah." I take another step toward him and his eyes warm even more.

"I also thought that I'd rather say hello than goodbye."

Oh, I like that. I can't help it, I give him a full-on grin.

His eyebrows rise and he gives me that supercilious look I'm so fond of.

"You're smiling at me," he says.

"I am." I keep smiling.

"I read the article you sent."

I take another step closer. Now we're only a breath apart, standing at the foot of the steps to my little cottage.

"What did you think?"

The air is thick and heavy between us. If I stood on my tiptoes I could press my lips to his. I could give him a swift kiss, as soft as the wings of a butterfly.

"I thought it was *interesting*," he says.

My heart gives a happy patter. "What did you like about it?" I whisper.

The article I wrote for him, listed all the reasons why Mariposa should be of interest to him. The sea, the turtles, the quaint cottages, the ordinary beauty of the island and most of all—

"I liked the bit where you said there's a woman there..."

"Who's waiting on a man," I say.

"To come and help paint her cottage," he says.

I reach up and cup my hand against his cheek and his eyes grow warmer. "Or take a walk on the beach."

"And go kayaking."

"Or watch a movie," I say.

"And make dinner together."

"All ordinary things," I say.

"That are made extraordinary because of you." He reaches up and rests his hand over mine. His touch travels through me, filling me with a fluttering of happiness.

"You recently said that nothing would induce you to like me—"

My chest tightens and I shake my head. "I'd take it back if I could. I'd take back so many things that I said."

"No. You were right. I was arrogant, rude, proud. My proposal..." He cuts off and looks to the side with a frown. "I'd take that back if I could. I'm surprised you didn't throw the teacake at me."

I laugh. "You would've caught it."

"What I was trying to say was that my heart was a better compass than all my logic and reason."

The sky is now pink and orange and is reflecting the exact shade of my happiness.

"I was wondering if I might try again," he says.

I give him a slow nod and try to contain the joy I'm feeling.

"Only if I'm allowed to try again too," I say.

"Naturally."

I grin at him.

"Isla?"

"Yes, Declan."

"I'd like very much if you'd agree to spend the rest of your life living a million little ordinary moments with me."

My mouth quivers as I try to hold back both a smile and tears.

"I don't know," I say, "I was sort of looking forward to the extraordinary. A private island, or a yacht, or maybe—"

He reaches down and grabs my arms. I squeal as he spins me around. "Is that so? You want extraordinary?"

I tilt my head back and laugh as we spin around my front garden.

Finally, Declan drops to the ground and I fall on top of him. I fit him just like I remember.

"I love you," he says.

It's just three ordinary words. I and love and you. But together they're extraordinary.

"I love you too," I say.

When I do, Declan pulls in a sharp breath. "I was hoping you'd say that."

Then his eyes widen. "What is this?"

I look up at the sunset painted sky. Above us are

thousands of delicate white butterflies flying over my wooded hill to find their beds for the night. Before they always looked like a snowstorm or a snow globe. But tonight they look like a thousand shooting stars for us to wish on.

"It's magic," I say.

Declan looks away from the butterflies and back to me. Finally he says, "That's what I thought too."

Then, he threads his hands through my hair and pulls me to him. When my mouth touches his, the butterflies disappear, the pink and orange sky disappears, everything disappears except the feel of him.

"Marry me," he whispers against my mouth.

I keep kissing him, caught up in the moment.

"Marry me," he demands.

I run my hands over his shoulders, down his chest, lower. He groans and grabs my wrists, stops my progress.

"Isla. Marry me."

There's the stern, commanding voice I love. I smile at the heat of his hands grasping me.

"Yes," I say.

At that, he flips me over, pushes me into the grass, and does all the delicious things I've fantasized about. All of them and more.

When we're done, I lie in his arms. The butterflies are gone and the moon has risen. Declan gently runs his hand over the edge of my breast.

"Do you think," I ask, "that we could do that again on the beach at Rosa? And the little island too?"

I look up and catch a grin on Declan's face.

"Oh, and also in a field in England. One of the grassy ones with sheep."

At that, he starts to laugh. It's rich and rumbly and sends a happy vibration through my whole body. I snuggle into him, catching his warmth.

"Does that mean yes?" I ask.

He kisses my temple. "That means I'll buy you the island, and the beach, and the field."

"Perfect," I say, giving him a blinding smile.

"Wonderful," he says.

And it is.

EPILOGUE

KATE'S VISION OF A WEDDING WITH HER, ME AND ARYA didn't come true. But Arya and Percy, and Declan and I, were all married in a small double ceremony on the beach.

Kate and Michael flew back to Mariposa and Renee took a day off work. My parents were there, and so was Declan's mom. Arya's whole family came, and so did Percy's.

Seagulls did make off with some of our wedding food, but none of us minded.

Kate's happy. Her family missed her as much as she missed them. She says that Michael is a charming husband, and she may hold onto him longer than a year or two. The way she says it, and the way they look at each other, makes me think it'll be a lot longer than only two years.

Renee finally made partner at her firm. She says that means she's also officially married.

Arya and Percy have decided to split time between Mariposa and England so that they can work on the conservation of both boobies and puffins. Especially because both birds mate for life.

It's a week after our wedding and Declan says that since I've nearly overcome my fear of flying, we can go wherever I'd like in the world. Live wherever I want. I tell him my home is my little cottage on Mariposa, but that I also really, really love his beautiful country estate.

"Of course you do," he says. "All gold diggers love country estates."

His eyes light with humor when he says this.

Unbelievable.

"Shut up and kiss me," I say.

So he does.

"Do you like that?" he asks.

I do. I like it.

No.

"I love it," I say.

"I love you," he says. Which makes me think of last night, and apricots, and lying down in the soft sand.

"I love you too."

Very, very much.

He must read the memory of last night in my eyes because he says, "I think we should stay on Mariposa a little longer."

I grin at him. "I agree. It's an interesting place."

"Very," he says.

We decide to forget about the future for now, instead

we'll go to the beach, for an ordinary, extraordinary walk in the moonlight.

We'll hold hands.

It'll be wonderful.

Really, really wonderful.

THE END

GET A BONUS EPILOGUE

Get an exclusive *Once Upon an Island* bonus epilogue for newsletter subscribers only!

When you join the Sarah Ready Newsletter you get access to sneak peaks, insider updates, exclusive bonus scenes and more.

Join Today!

www.sarahready.com/newsletter

ABOUT THE AUTHOR

Author Sarah Ready writes contemporary romance and romantic comedy. Her books have been described as "euphoric", "heartwarming" and "laugh out loud". Her debut novel *The Fall in Love Checklist* was hailed as "the unicorn read of 2020".

Sarah writes stand-alone romcoms and romcoms in the Soulmates in Romeo series, all of which can be found at her website: www.sarahready.com.

Stay up to date, get exclusive epilogues and bonus content. Join Sarah's newsletter at www.sarahready.com/newsletter.

ALSO BY SARAH READY

Stand Alone Romances:

The Fall in Love Checklist

Hero Ever After

Josh and Gemma Make a Baby

Soul Mates in Romeo Romance Series:

Chasing Romeo

Love Not at First Sight

Romance by the Book

Love, Artifacts, and You

Married by Sunday

Stand Alone Novella:

Love Letters

Find these books and more by Sarah Ready at:

www.sarahready.com/romance-books